THE KING OF CARCOSA

THE FINAL BOOK OF LOST CARCOSA

JOSEPH SALE

ISBN: 978-1-940250-69-4

Cover Art by Mushfiq A.K.

Interior Layout by Lori Michelle
  www.TheAuthorsAlley.com

Printed in the United States of America

Visit us on the web at:
www.bloodboundbooks.net
https://www.bloodgutsandstory.com/

"The Horizon of all Consciousness is focused in the Perfection of Sentience; all things are chanced for the Realisation of I: the Self as Magick Entire."

—*The Dragon Book of Essex,* Andrew D. Chumbley

CHAPTER 1
THE PILGRIM

THE PILGRIM SAID, "O Great King, who has gone beyond the pillars of eternity, who has touched the untouchable mystery, please tell me: what is this place? And what, if you know the answer, is Death?"

The King pondered for a moment, and then said, "Dear Pilgrim, who hath journeyed long, endured much travail and hardship, for thine own sake and for others, know that this place is the Underworld, the place of those who are dead . . . " The King's eyes gleamed with effulgent light. "But know also, that Death is simply an illusion."

"An illusion? But Great King, how can that be so? For I have tasted the pain of Death. I have felt its scorpion sting."

"Have you, indeed? How comes it then that we are here, conversing? How comes it then that thou art not destroyed? Was it truly *thee* that suffered the pain of Death, or was it not merely thy body? When the leaves of the tree fall, does the tree die? When the urn full of water is struck by the hammer and breaks, is the water damaged as it pours out from the broken vessel?"

The Pilgrim considered the King's words.

"Then, do you say I am eternal?"

The King smiled beneath his hood.

"Verily, I say to thee: thou art eternal."

"Are all men eternal?"

"Yes. Though the nature of their eternity differs."

The Pilgrim's face shadowed.

"Do you speak of heaven and hell?"

"Perhaps."

"Are we in heaven?"

3

"No.

"Then surely this must be hell?"

"No.

"Then we are between, in purgatory, or perhaps limbo?"

"Thou reachest for false certainties. There is only one certainty, and that is thy consciousness. Thou art the all-pervading Observer, the Grand Knower, the Watchman. As am I. As all souls are."

"You and I are One then?" The Pilgrim looked pleased by this revelation.

The King smiled again.

"All things are One. To speak of 'thou' or 'I' is mere fantasy, though a necessary fantasy until thou see for thyself."

"Am I ready to see?"

The King's eyes glimmered, and the face long hidden beneath the cowl—which in truth was no physical adornment but a spiritual occlusion—became grave.

"Thou hast little choice. Death has led you to this moment. Either way, thou will cast off thy illusions. There is no choice in that. Only, the *manner* in which thou cast them off."

The Pilgrim nodded, though the King wondered if he truly understood.

"You are speaking of that other world?"

"Yes."

"The place I was before?"

"Yes."

"I see now that such a place was also mere illusion."

"Thou hast learned quickly. But now, I shall question thee: knowing thy former existence to be illusion, and knowing Death also to be illusion, what should thou doest? Reject thy former, illusory existence and embrace non-existence?"

The Pilgrim pondered for long moments.

"No. For one can only reject something that exists."

The King laughed loud and long.

"Thou art a good pupil."

"You are a better teacher."

"If thou wilst not reject the illusion, then I suppose thou shall embrace it then, rejecting non-existence and returning to existence?

The Pilgrim shook his head.

"That doesn't work either, for then I shall simply be caught in more illusions."

The King concealed his secret joy.

"Then thou will doest nothing, neither rejecting nor embracing the illusion . . . ?" The King allowed the suggestion to hover, testing the Pilgrim a third and final time.

"No," the Pilgrim said, quite firmly. "For to perceive a difference between inaction and action is also an illusion."

The King bowed his head.

"Thou hast become the master, and I the pupil."

"We are One," the Pilgrim said, happily. "But now you must help me. Suppose I was to return to the illusion, to fulfil the karmic debt I owed to it, suppose there was a way, how might I continue to function and fulfil my purpose, knowing all to be illusion?"

The King considered the question thoughtfully.

"Thou wilst appear, to all others, as an ordinary man, acting in accordance with his will. But beneath, in thy most secret heart of hearts, thou shalt know the world for what it is, thou shalt detach thyself from the tyranny of outcomes, and reject the poison of worldly consolations."

"If I reject the tyranny of outcomes, how then shall I know right from wrong?"

"Both are illusions."

"How then shall I decide upon a course of action?"

"Thou forgettest already that thou art not the ship, that must decide to plot its course east or west, north or south; thou art the sea itself, endless, immortal, and purer than diamond."

The Pilgrim wept.

"With this Truth comes the destruction of all that is wicked."

"This is so. And thus, the decision is made for thee."

The Pilgrim nodded. "I see that now."

The King saddened.

"It is almost time, dear Pilgrim."

The Pilgrim looked into the King's gleaming yellow eyes, saw his sorrow, and was almost moved again to tears by it.

"I am grateful, so grateful . . . "

"Thou art welcome." The King paused. "Such attachments are soon to leave me forever, dear Pilgrim. And so I would ask a favour of thee, before thou goest."

"Anything."

"My daughter, when thou seest her, tell her I love her and I shall miss her, but that one day, she shall see me again, when the last veil of illusion falls from her eyes . . . Tell her . . . No, that is enough."

"I will tell her." The Pilgrim bowed. "But tell me: shall I then return?"

"My dear Abracadabra, what could be more certain?"

CHAPTER 2
WARPATH

DESIRE DROVE HER like the whip of a slaver; and indeed, Desire was her new master. Though she had been crowned the Demon Queen, though she had conquered the Six-Ringed City, though she had laid her enemy low, still she felt Desire's whip upon her back, and knew deep down, in the darkest recesses of her heart, that she was not yet free.

She rode upon Satan out of the eternal gates of the Six-Ringed City, the watchtower's unseen trumpet—forged from a substance unknown even to the eldest of the black planet—sounding high and clear, a song of victory. She had forgiven her steed for his cowardice, but in her own mind she knew that a third betrayal would mean the creature's death.

Above her flew the trueborn. Though many had been lost in the civil war, their numbers were still sufficient to darken the sky. Black pinions beat the air, producing the sound of a hurricane. Their gleaming flesh and weaponry, all colours of the rainbow, set the clouds afire with new spectrums. There was Malebolge, the Cruel. De'katan, the Relentless. Ashe'oken, the Unparalleled.

In truth, none were as strong in battle as Ashe'non, nor as cunning as Kal'darion, nor as loyal as Lath'lelin. But it mattered not. The great Pe'karians had been slain in the latest civil war or the many battles with Carcosa before it. The time of legendary soldiers was at an end. Her success rested not on the shoulders of mortals, but on the foundation of the Self.

She smiled darkly.

Before Alan Chambers, there had been Andrew. Fiery, sulphuric Andrew. He had been a promising candidate for the champion she'd sought to fashion, only he had rather too much

THE KING OF CARCOSA

Will. Headstrong, brilliant, a natural syncretic thinker. He'd mastered magic in mere months, achieved greatness within the year. Indeed, *she'd* learned a few things from *him*. But then he began to see things his own way. She'd cut him down in his thirty-seventh year. His books survived him. A few copies even circulated the world he had left, Earth. They contained glimpses of Carcosa for one who knew where to look.

It was Andrew who had reminded her, after long eons of frustration and failure, that reliance on the Self was the only reliance. All other things were transitory illusions. She saw that more clearly now than ever. Alan Chambers was not a person—not real, not in truth—but rather a mechanism of self-actualisation created by the universe for *her,* no more substantial than the phantoms of Demhe.

It was many days' march before her army reached the border between the lands of Blue Light and Demhe. The army was unruly, composed as it were a mixture of elements: infantry, gorgonopsid calvary, trueborn elite, and horrors dredged from the chasmal depths of Pe'kar's dungeons. Some of these experiments were monstrous in form—squidlike compositions of restless flesh. Others looked human, could be conversed with perfectly rationally, but hid within them strange powers of healing or harm. Many hybrids also accompanied the host, therianthropic beings that looked as though they had crawled out from the bottomless well of Greek mythology—indeed, perhaps that had been Pe'kar's inspiration. Bull-men, tigress-women, crow-winged archers, frontrunners whose flesh and brains had been removed and grafted to the skeletons of horses. These disturbing centaurs—though in truth they were homunculi—galloped ahead of the pack, scouting with roaming eyes, their human faces cantilevered from swollen, hairless horse-bodies. The sight of them repulsed her, but they were effective, their gangly limbs moving at a rapid canter.

And of course, the army's crowning jewel: a dark, gorgeously ornate ark fashioned from indignite and sealed with a spell, in which was housed The Claw. She thought of the ark as Alan's funeral bier. Indeed, she did not intend to use The Claw in any battle strategy. She brought it with her purely for symbolic purposes—and to ensure its destruction at journey's end. *Then the last trace of him will be gone.* The thought brought her some sadness.

At the threshold between the lands of Blue Light and Demhe, she beheld the two pillars raised in the image of the fell constellation of Two Towers; beyond it, the desert lay vast, vapid, and still. Where once its dunes had seemed to swell and shift like waves, now they stood like barrows, abandoned hills entombing the silent dead. Not even the revenants of those graves stirred. No ghost of her father, nor of her mother. No remonstrations from those she had lost, betrayed, or slain. She had been preparing herself for a confrontation with Alan Chamber's shade—a chance to kill him again, perhaps—but it seemed she would be denied that pleasure. Demhe had given up its dreaming. *Now, the universe bends to my will,* she thought. *For the first time, luck and fate are on my side.* The way lay open to march across the sands. Her destination was ultimately Carcosa, but not at first.

Before Cali could unite the black planet, and claim her kingdom once and for all, she wanted *revenge.* That was the true Desire burning in her heart, driving her onward with the cruelty of a slave-master. That Desire perhaps raged more ferociously now than even her Desire for victory. She rationalised it was logical to tie up the loose ends, to be rid of the last magicians who might oppose her, but deep down she knew that it was not strategy directing her steps, but hunger—all-consuming as a great serpent.

The march eastward would take her army to the slopes of Al Qaf Saba.

The Emerald Mountain would burn red.

CHAPTER 3
THE TRIO

WHAT SHOULD WE *do now?* The question was on all of their minds, but none had spoken it aloud. Days had passed without being marked. The desire for all worldly things—even sustenance—had left them. Cassilda felt that they were in some kind of limbo. And she thought this world—Urth—was grey enough to be the realm between life and death. Enough rage and fire burned in her to let her know she was not dead yet, but equally, she felt like her heart was no longer beating. Time was just for killing.

She stepped outside *The Black Star* and walked the streets of a nameless little town. The buildings looked squat and ugly to her: prosaic mausoleums to dead imagination. Ugly vehicles moved to and fro over grey roads like mindless beetles.

Alan came here, she thought. *One dark and stormy night. Or maybe it was bright and sunny?* There was so much she didn't know. Alan's life had been a form of lie, according to Master Hao, but then again, it had also been true. He had believed in his life, and so it had become real. Who knew how many lifetimes Alan had lived out in this world, reincarnating himself, believing each new version to be isolated, finite, limited. The thought made Cassilda so heavy with sadness she had to drag her feet like leaden weights across the pavement. *If only you could have realised who you truly were, if only you could have believed.* The truth had been revealed to Alan, but some final step had been missing, and enlightenment failed to find him. Or he it. However these things worked.

Cassilda, of course, understood magic at a deep level. She comprehended the theory but knew the practice of that final illumination was beyond her. She would never be able to rise to the level of her father, or to the level Alan could have aspired to; she was altogether too bound up in her head, too intellectual, and too fond of control. To become the instrument of the universe, one had to abandon the sense of "doing", and simply allow things to happen . . . She had perhaps endured too much trauma for that.

Except, Alan helped you. With him, you could let go.

More than once, tears flowed as she walked. They burned scars into her cheeks, red tattoos that made her look like the tribal warriors of ancient lore. She drew attention from passersby—she was, after all, still glad in shimmering robes, the hem of which was dipped in blood, and there was an aura about her that made one think of electricity dancing between clouds—but none felt brave enough to approach, except the odd lecher, thinking her a vulnerable, slight woman. When they saw her eyes, they quickly departed, realising that things would not go their way should they try anything.

Petruccio and LeBarron were coping little better than she. There was a small consolation in sharing her grief with others who knew something of its depth. The actor was despondent, almost suicidal, Cassilda thought. Petruccio was impassive as always, though his stoniness no longer seemed like strength, more a terrible brittleness that would shatter at any moment.

They could not keep going as they were. But nor could they think how to move forward. All of them seemed unconsciously aware of this fact. And eventually, chance conspired to bring them together, sitting in one of the many dark rooms that made up *The Black Star's* compact underworld.

The room was stone-walled, lit by braziers, much like the ritual room in which Alan had been initiated long ago, only it was not so open and bare, sporting a long table in its centre and tapestries on its walls. *The Black Star's* supply rooms still held frozen foods, and Petruccio spontaneously cooked them all a thick, glutenous supper. They ate it without hunger or pleasure around the table, firelight painting their faces into the glowering countenances of demons—rebel angels holding council in the low courts of Pandemonium. *Hell is better than Limbo,* Cassilda thought. *At least in hell, I might feel something.*

For a long time, none spoke, eating in grim silence. Finally, it was LeBarron who broke the black enchantment.

"We can't let Cali win."

"Nor can we beat her," Petruccio said. "At least, not by any way I can think of."

LeBarron looked at his sword, which sat like a discarded relic in the corner of the room, its fell metallurgy winking in the flame-light.

"That sword could cut her."

"I have no doubt of that," Petruccio said. "Only that you would never get close enough to do so. You saw her power, her aura. Only Alan could stand up to it."

"Or my father," Cassilda said, tonelessly. The others both knew she was not speaking from a place of hope, only deeper despair. Whereas she had once entertained the idea her father might return, now she was certain he was dead. Cali had won.

"And Pe'kar," Petruccio said, hopelessness unable to quash his thoroughness. "So, in other words, the three who could have stood against her are gone."

"There must be a way," LeBarron said. "Cali *herself* overturned established order. She slew Pe'kar. Surely *that* would have been considered impossible, once upon a time?"

"There are weapons that can kill gods," Cassilda said. Bitterly, she thought of The Claw. If they still had The Claw, then one of them might have made the ultimate sacrifice, severing their own hand and taking up its mantle, but Cali had even robbed them of that vain hope. All was ruin. Hopes cast into the abyss. She still saw Alan falling away from them, headless, in her dreams. Sometimes, she saw it just as it had happened. Other times, a great serpent waited in the blackness, opening its mouth to swallow Alan whole.

"In the vaults of the palace," Petruccio said. "But who has the knowledge and skill to fashion one?"

There were blacksmiths, artificers, and bowyers galore in Carcosa, but none, Cassilda thought, who knew the secrets of reversing immortality. How had Cali herself known? Had Pe'kar revealed to her a secret that would prove his own undoing? Had her father, hoping she would one day slay His enemy? Or had Cali discovered the secret for herself. One thing Cassilda could not take away from her sister was she, unlike Cassilda, had the true magician's mind, a mind of relentless exploration and inquiry that sought to unravel the Gordian knots of reality. *And yet, for all your curiosity, you are closed, Cali. Why didn't you take my offer? Why didn't you take the way of peace?*

Cassilda knew the answer, though the pain of it was almost too great to bear.

"We might at least try," LeBarron said. "Perhaps, with my dreaming blood, I might—"

Cassilda slammed her fist upon the table. "Stop pretending you're him!"

Silence followed, though the stones themselves seemed to ring.

LeBarron held up his hands, surprisingly meek. "I would never make such a claim. I was only trying give us hope . . . "

"Hope is treacherous," Petruccio said. "But there is no sense in giving up. Millions of souls dwell in Carcosa, and if we abandon them now, Cali will truly have won. It may be we die, but we cannot leave the city to torment and ruin. Your father made me Head Courtier, and I intend to earn a little bit of that title. I would rather die upon its walls than here, knowing I was a coward when it mattered most."

A strange fire lived in the dwarf's eyes. Not the burning flame of some impassioned youth, but the superheated magma that ran beneath the earth's crust, stone itself boiling to a bright, incandescent river.

Cassilda felt her heart hammer at his words. An energy surged up her spine, through her fingertips. Her skin goosefleshed.

"Yes," she muttered. "Yes, that is the way to die, isn't it? Spitting in her face."

Petruccio grinned. "Now *that* is the princess I have so come to admire."

LeBarron looked grey and grave, older than he had ever seemed.

"I would rather not die a third time. But then again, what is life without death? Our world decays because tyrants cannot die . . . Only, who will remember the actor? The man upon the stage is merely an illusion, a shadow. They will remember the masks but not the face. Remember the dance, but not the ones who made the steps." LeBarron stared into some nothingness visible only to him. Cassilda wondered if he saw that mystical realm that lay beyond death, a realm he had already glimpsed at least once.

Cassilda did not reach out and touch his hand, that would have been too familiar, but she smiled sadly.

"I do not believe that will be your destiny, LeBarron. Perhaps all of us will be forgotten for a time, if Cali does hold sway, but perhaps not . . . Stories live on in the most unexpected ways. And the truth always seems to have its day." Those last words were a sour taste in her mouth, because she had still declined to share with LeBarron the fate of The Stranger, the one whom he worshipped and adored so zealously.

The actor was smiling back at her.

"You are a poet, dear princess! O, for all my swordplay, I was not made for war. What I would give to live in a time of peace, of song-writing and lovemaking! Those were the stars I was born under, not labyrinths and crumbling towers . . . "

"Those times will come again," Petruccio said. "And we have a chance to make it so. Though success is slim, we must give our all. We return to Carcosa and open the vaults. Whatever horrors and dark materials dwell there, we shall fashion them into a weapon that might wound Cali . . . "

LeBarron jumped up, as though receiving an electric shock. He looked like a galvanised corpse. Though sorrow and exhaustion still hung over him from their many ordeals, transcendent energy animated his inner being.

"Then we need a name!"

"I beg your pardon?" Cassilda asked confused.

"A name!" LeBarron said. "Come, a sorceress must know better than most that there's power in a name, power in words. Cali is the Demon Queen, the Destroyer, the Black Empress—these are her names and they give her power. What are we? LeBarron, Petruccio, and Cassilda? That is not enough. We need a name, something that will give her pause, something that people will remember!"

Cassilda smiled.

"I like your style," she said, "but imagination was never my strong point." *It was Alan's—born out of his weird and eclectic desires. Dreaming was in his blood in so many ways.*

"I have it," Petruccio said. "We shall be *Il Triello*."

The other two frowned, confused.

"I think I know the answer to this question before I ask it," Petruccio said. "But nonetheless, I shall ask. When I lived here, I was fond of a special art-form called 'movies'. Westerns always caught my fancy. I don't suppose either of you have seen The *Good, The Bad, and The Ugly*?"

"I do not know anything about this art-form you call 'movie'," Cassilda said, archly.

"Imagine one of LeBarron's plays but recorded as a series of moving images grafted to special paper. This paper can have light projected through it, which illuminates the images in rapid succession, 'performing' the play before an audience." Petruccio turned to LeBarron. "In other words, LeBarron, we might record one of your greatest ever performances, and that performance would be set in amber for all of time. You could re-watch that exact same performance as many times as you wish. It would never change provided it had been accurately recorded. That is what the people of Earth call 'movies' or 'films'."

"Alan alluded to these once or twice," Cassilda said, with a sad smile. "But I did not understand his meaning. I thank you, Petruccio, for giving me a little more insight into the man I . . . " She could not finish the sentence.

Petruccio bowed.

LeBarron bit his lip, shifted foot to foot.

"I am not sure how I feel about a film . . . " the actor said. "On the one hand, it would be glorious to have the same immortalisation as a poet or writer . . . But on the other hand, the life of the play is in the moment, the exquisite point of power that exists in the *now*. The connection between player and played, audience and actor, the space that exists between destroyed by the intimacy and immediacy of the thing . . . I don't know how that could ever be recreated."

"It can't," Petruccio acknowledged. "But there are other advantages. A film can be refined and perfected in the same way that a script can be endlessly re-written in order to improve it."

"I see," LeBarron said. "But curious as this is, what relationship does it have to your name, *Il Triello?*"

"There is a film that is very famous in this world called *The Good, The Bad, and The Ugly*." Petruccio was smiling now. "It is about three very dangerous men on a quest to find buried gold, though of course the gold is symbolic of something deeper. One of the men is good, one bad, and one ugly, though one can never be *quite* sure which is which. These three titanic forces continue to orbit each other, until finally they must meet in a cataclysmic showdown . . . "

Cassilda smiled, cottoning on.

"So you are saying that we are the good, the bad, and the ugly?"
Petruccio nodded.

"And the great confrontation awaits us?" LeBarron said.
Petruccio nodded again.

"The trio, *il triello,* were working at odds—but we are united. We represent the union of these three forces. And who knows, maybe that union is enough to stop the Demon Queen?"

LeBarron smiled.

"I like how you think, Petruccio. The union of three forces. I like it."

"Me too," Cassilda said. *Alan would approve, in so many ways.*

"Well then, it is settled," Petruccio said.

"There is just one thing I would like to know," Cassilda said.

"Oh?"

"When these three dangerous men—the good, the bad, and the ugly—meet: what happens?"

Petruccio smiled grimly.

"One of them dies."

CHAPTER 4
THE GARDEN

THERE WAS A garden into which he, himself, entered.

Abracadabra found himself lost in childlike wonder as the beauty of this secret place unfolded around him, dazzling senses that he thought no longer existed. The canopy of trees was a translucent shadow-play of most intricate patterning, the vein-like latticework of branches forming Rorschach patterns that impressed a variety of forms and spectres upon his imagination. The last daylight broke through gaps, a light of many colours that seemed to cause chemical reactions wherever it strayed. Grass sprouted with renewed intensity beneath its beam. Flowers changed their shape and hues. Tree-trunks were painted with glyphs, which seemed to open, revealing secret doorways to inner kingdoms. Birds of paradise flitted between extended branches. The earth beneath his feet was soft like down.

Flowers erupted everywhere, a variety so infinite that he gave up categorising them. Most common, however, was a genus that grew five finger-like petals reaching for the stars; they were deep purple in colour, their pollen-rich centre—for bees were everywhere in this mysterious place, but especially upon these flowers—glowing faintly, as though with an inner radiance. Unmistakably they resembled hands.

Abracadabra examined himself and found that he now had two hands, where in another lifetime one had been severed from him, and he wept, realising his wholeness.

"Do you miss The Claw?"

The voice came from somewhere behind him, but he was not startled. The King was always with him, and there was a comfort in that.

THE KING OF CARCOSA

Abracadabra considered for a moment, then he nodded.

"Further evidence, if any were needed, that thy work is not yet done," the King said. "But come, what is it about The Claw that has thee longing for brighter flowers than those blooming in Eden?"

"With The Claw I felt powerful. I felt . . . " He reached for a concept that was increasingly becoming irrelevant and useless, as his memory of what went before dimmed. It was like watching a lit candle in the bow of a funeral boat drift slowly away upon dark waters—the memory of who lay in the boat fading with the light as it was carried beyond sight and mind. " . . . I felt like a man."

"Does power define what it is to be a man?" There was a hardness to the King's questioning, though also compassion.

"Not necessarily." Abracadabra tore his eyes away from the hand-flowers. Above them, birdsong filled the trees; an evening song, he thought, sweet and yet sorrowful. "But when I held The Claw, I felt that nothing was beyond my reach.

"Nothing is beyond thy reach," The King replied. "That is verily the truth. The Claw is just another illusion. But of course, illusions can sometimes lead us to the truth."

"You speak as though from experience. Yet tell me, O Great King, what illusions could you have possibly overcome? I struggle to believe that at one point your eyes were not open, as now."

The King began to walk through the garden, and Abracadabra fell naturally into step. Around them, the garden's secret inhabitants continued their strange dance, the song deepening and deepening in melodic complexity, other voices answering it from far away, the night-flowers unfurling their clandestine hearts, hearts that opened only to the moon. It was as though this ritual, this dance of life, *created* the night, rather than merely precipitated it. Night was this dance; this dance was night.

They stepped through an avenue of roses curled into arches—though with no visible means of support, past beds of towering succulents, and into a little glade pierced by starlight. Spiders diligently wove webs of pure silver. Fox eyes stared out from the secrecy of shrubs. The air was redolent of sweet wine, a headiness that was almost overpowering, yet just when its intoxication seemed too much, the senses were refreshed by a gust of light, clear breeze.

"The moment of enlightenment eradicates all other moments," The King said, thoughtfully. "In truth, there is no moment. We are

18

born and die enlightened, born and die knowing the truth—but we deny it, push it down, obscure it with illusions."

"Like death?"

"Yes, like death. If thou livest thy life in fear of death, dost thou live at all? Thus, the illusion of death clouds the truth of life."

Abracadabra was suddenly struck by inspiration as to the King's meaning. "And The Claw, it clouds the truth of power?"

The King nodded.

"The power is within thee, but so long as thou clingest to the talisman of power, rather than power itself, thou shalt not know it."

"So I needed to lose The Claw to harness the pigment?"

"Thou speakest still too literally of things. To thee, the pigment is a substance, like the blood that once flowed through the veins of thy mortal body. But it is not substance, nor even essence—far more elusive, far more precious. A connection to something higher." The King lifted his gaze to the wonders around them, and it seemed his gaze—like the starlight—inspired change in the garden. A tree that Abracadabra had thought was covered in hanging silver buds revealed its true nature: the temple of a thousand chrysalises, each hatching as the King lifted a sparkling hand, and let out a laugh that was as honey-sweet as any sound he had ever heard. The butterflies burst into life, colours and eyes dancing through the air, and then rose into the sky. The silence of their wingbeats was a music Abracadabra thirsted to hear once more.

After a long while had passed, both drinking in the stillness, Abracadabra said, "You have been here many times before."

"I first learned how when I was an infant in the grand scheme of the cosmos." The King began to walk again, Abracadabra falling into step. What new wonders would the garden reveal? He could spend an eternity here. For some reason, that thought did not trouble him. "My brother came with me, then. We were not always enemies . . . " The King sighed and a jolt of fear had passed through Abracadabra.

"Your brother . . . is he . . . here then?"

The King shook his head.

"No. He forfeited that right long ago, though in truth reaching this place is not so hard. Not the first time. But getting *back* . . . now that takes a rare magician."

THE KING OF CARCOSA

"I am not a magician."

"Art thou not? Hast thou not outwitted a demon and claimed the magical talisman he guarded? Hast thou not persuaded madmen back into sanity? Nursed sick men back into health? Hast thou not defeated thy many enemies with a mere wave of thy hand? Didst thou not attain the revelation of thy true being? And commit the final sorcerous leap of the magician—the leap into the abyss—casting aside the world of flesh in favour of the eternal spirit?" The King smiled without physical motion, only a deeper radiance. "Thou art a magician indeed."

Abracadabra halted, and the King graciously paused. The two faced one another, and it seemed the whole garden—which had no limits—was listening.

"Then I must go back, like you said before. I must . . . return to the other place."

"Yes. But first, thou must meet thy peers."

Abracadabra blinked. The King had vanished, leaving him alone in the garden.

Night came on like a slow serpent.

CHAPTER 5
DARKNESS HAS FALLEN
ON THE FLOWERS

T HE SLOPES OF the Emerald Mountain were covered in bright Alyssas and Aarons, waving in a breeze that was hot and sweet. But the dazzling display left no impression upon Cali. She looked upon the mountain as a hateful enemy. Her time there had been ruinous to her pride, a humiliation she'd scarcely recovered from. The elation of having found the mountain had soon been dashed by her failure to complete the trial. Knowledge of the pigment would forever remain tantalisingly out of reach.

No. You shall claim by force what was denied you then.

Their system was flawed anyway. It denied progress. For, did not every soul grow and improve over the course of their life? Why should one only be allowed to attempt to claim the pigment once? Surely, seekers should be allowed to return and try again when they had bettered themselves? Cali's life had been long, and she had learned much. *Though in the last few months, you have learned more than in the millennia preceding it.* True enough. She had Alan Chambers to thank for that. Oh how she wished she could have caught his head before it fell, so that she could have claimed his skull as an ornament. He would have made an amusing travelling companion, a poor Yorick to unburden her inner world to. There was no one else whom she felt worthy of such an honour.

The image of Alan's skull brought to Cali's mind the memory of a painting; a dark, shadowy mirage of a portrait that showed a skull-face emerging from the waters of some cosmic soup. Everything slanted and chaotic. All definite lines on the verge of dissolution. A masterpiece, in its own disturbing way, a vision of

21

the death's head that existed behind the mask all mortals wore as a face.

Yes, before Andrew, there had been Austin. Brilliant, kind, fearless, pleasure-obsessed Austin. He desired nothing more than to make love to death's image. His fantasy was the Crone, and Cali had adopted that guise all too readily, relishing in the theatrics. How much more fascinating was Austin's fetish than the standard longings of mortal men for youthful, submissive women. No, Austin's desires were as strange and deep as his magical practice—he was one of the few magicians she had schooled in her long quest to find a malleable champion who had been totally unafraid to plumb the depths of his own unconscious.

A pity how it had to end . . .

Unlike Andrew, whose rapid rise to power and mastery of magic—combined with a fierce independence—made him dangerous, Austin had proved more useful to her, working for her cause over a number of decades. But in time, his obsession with forms of sexual transgression and ascension led him to quite literal bestiality. She had found him more than once returning, pale faced and bloodied, from a journey into the marshes, not to hunt beasts but to *seduce* them. If she had not been so impressed by the courage of his perversions, she might have felt disgust. Desire, which had made Austin's magic so powerful, ultimately proved his undoing, destroying his body through disease and expended energies. A sad fate for one with so much promise.

She shook herself. The memories of these men felt like ghosts, the last remnants of an old snake-skin still clinging to her shining new scales. This was the second time she had thought about one of her previous champions. Before this week, she had not thought of them in long decades.

Satan snarled and pawed the ground, eager to be on the move, eager to assail the mountain. She felt his hunger as a rippling energy that travelled up and down his spine.

Her army seemed equally restless. The camp was alive with activity: ring-fighting, gambling, orgies, and ritualistic preparations for the war to come; she tolerated their hedonisms with as much indifference as she could muster. Unlike Pe'kar, she knew that true power came neither from asceticism nor indulgence but something that lay between both. The soldiers in her army had lived most of their lives either imprisoned by Pe'kar's strictures or else literally imprisoned in his dark laboratories. She offered them freedom, and allowing them to exorcise that freedom would garner further loyalty.

Despite that, soon she would have to set them loose on something, if only to return their focus. But not yet. First, she wanted to approach the mountain herself. She wanted to confront the ancient curmudgeon who guarded the secret temple, to make him kiss her feet before stamping him out of existence forever.

She dismounted.

"Stay," she commanded. Satan inclined his head and snorted, though his eyes gleamed with something that might have been irritation.

Cali left her army and began to walk up the mountain slope.

The path of flowers was long and winding. The mountain lay eerily silent save for wind stirring the innumerable blossoms. Petals of every colour flashed with radiance. Stems and branches of every type tangled in complexities that seemed more pattern or language than accident of nature. Thorns winked in the light of the twin suns. The stone from which the mountain itself had been reared glowed a deep, dark emerald. There was something simultaneously foreboding and inviting about that colour, like peering into the heart of a lover, unsure what one might find.

Ahead, she spotted the cave mouth, a dark slit that promised the fecund potential of something newly born. A tangible darkness breathed within. Though she had risen to the heights of deity, yet she felt a subtle tremor of fear. She knew the man who kept the mountain; he was no god, but nor was he to be trifled with. Many great warriors, wizards, and women of power had come before him and been broken. This was not a fight she instigated lightly. But it had to be done. Her new inner god, Desire, demanded it.

She permitted herself one last look back before entering Al Qaf Saba. She saw her army arrayed at the foot of the mountain, like a great ant-hive marching to war, circled by potent hornets. The army stretched far, far into the desert, carpeting gold in black. How would Carcosa, weakened and devoid of leadership, possibly stand against her? And had Pe'kar been blind or stupid not to see victory had been within his grasp long centuries ago?

Her eyes were drawn eastward. Though it was the faintest of mirages, the gossamer whisper of a dream—perhaps, she thought with sardonic relish, the last dream Demhe would ever offer up—

she could make out the spires and crenulations of profane, hideous, wondrous Carcosa. Yes, even now it made the hairs stand on her arm. She understood Pe'kar's jealousy. The land of Blue Light, for all its foreboding strangeness, was nothing next to the splendour and horror of Dim Carcosa. She would possess the city of her father, or be utterly destroyed.

"Soon," she whispered.

She stepped into the cave's darkness, following the strange tunnel. It wound, serpentine, narrowing and narrowing almost to the level she was forced to turn sideways on. *How undignified,* she thought. *Does the mountain seek to humble me?* If the mountain tried to crush her, she would crack it to the foundations, shatter the emerald stone and scatter its rubble to the four corners of the black planet.

Deeper and deeper the tunnel wound. She expected the light of Hao's eternally burning fire, but it was absent. Therefore it took her a few moments to realise she had reached the main chamber. Her eyes, gifted with nightvision, adjusted instantly to the penumbra. She saw clearly the art daubed upon the cave walls—such things had once fascinated and inspired her, but now she sickened of art. Once Carcosa fell under her rule, she might risk a journey back to Earth simply to obliterate all of Petruccio's paintings. The act was petty and spiteful, and she knew it, but she wanted no trace of the artist's vanity left in the world she would build.

"So, you have finally come back," a voice said from the shadows.

Cali snarled. Somehow, she was not able to see the old master, even with her supra-normal eyesight. Hao had a knack for invisibility, for cloaks and deceptions. This chamber was his, and here his illusions were at their most powerful.

"Do not pretend you have foreseen this moment!" Cali spat. "You are not so wise as that. You hid this place from Pe'kar for a long time, but you cannot hide it from me."

Fire burst into life. Cali recoiled, her hand going to her side, where the deadly blade that had cut the head from Alan Chamber's shoulder still hung. It had taken every ounce of willpower to wash his blood from the blade.

The flamelight illuminated a wizened, ancient face. Though at first it appeared to be the face of a man with Asiatic features, soon the illusion began to shift, the amiable exterior giving lie to something black and shining beneath, the way a silken cloth conceals the poisoned dagger blade.

"But I did foresee this moment," he said. "And every moment else to come. Such is the joy of being One with the One."

"There is no One," Cali snapped. "That was a superstition my father too readily believed."

"Or perhaps he knew something you do not."

"Do not dare utter the word 'God' in my presence, Hao. I am God. Or the closest thing that the black planet will ever see to it."

Hao sighed. His dark, beady eyes never gave Cali the courtesy of attention, but rested only on the flame. He looked, for all intents and purposes, like a wizened man, sat plumply upon a log, no more threatening than an overfed chaffinch. But his emerald and purple robes glistened with the same predatory quality of scales beneath the surface of water; his aura practically reeked of magic. Cali would not let her guard down for one moment.

"If you are in a talking mood, then let us talk," Hao said.

His informal, amiable manner irritated her beyond words, but she thought of his manner as desperation, a final ego-trip before his inevitable extinction. Viewing his insults as a mere expression of his mortal frailty, she found she could just about hold her anger in check. *See how I have grown!*

"What do we have to talk about?"

"God. The pigment. Whatever you wish. I assume you have come here to kill me. Therefore, you might as well get as much wisdom out of me as you can."

"There is no wisdom in you, nor the serpentkin. Only folly."

At last, he looked at her. It grated her to know she found his stare difficult to hold.

"If that is so, then why did you come to us?"

"I came seeking a promise that was a lie."

"There was no lie," he countered. "The pigment is real, and had you passed the test . . . "

"The test?" Cali laughed, though she hated how forced it was. "Psychosexual parlour tricks. Antiquated ideas of asceticism. Is that what amounts to magic in your sad, isolated circle?" Cali grinned, resembling a hyena stumbling upon the carcass of a proud lion in its death throes. "I will show you true magic."

Hao made a soft noise. It might have been *hmm*. Or perhaps

Hrmpf. Either way, it made Cali's blood boil. To make matters worse, he had returned to gazing into the fire, as though losing interest in her.

"You know I have an army at my back," she said. "I can raze this place to the ground. But if you tell me what you should have told me all those years ago, if you reveal to me the location of the pigment, and its secret, I could find mercy in my heart."

"Mercy is given freely. Like love. But these are two things you know nothing about."

Cali's lip curled. Her fists were clenched so tightly she felt that she was becoming stone herself.

"And what do you know of love? A hermit, living in a cave in the mountain—in the middle of a desert! You devoted your life to Uboth and the pigment. I doubt you have ever lain with a man or woman, unless the serpentkin satisfy your needs. I would not put it past them, for clearly sex is ever on their minds; why else would they devise such a crude trial for the pigment?" She sneered, but Hao remained unmoved. "I asked you a question, old man. What could *you* possibly know about love, about passion? I have loved and lost. I have known the death of those I hold dear."

"Caused."

"I'm sorry?"

"You have *caused* the death of those you hold dear."

Cali felt herself turning white—her rage was an icy spear piercing her spine.

"I will only give you one more chance, Hao. Mock me, and I shall send you to a grave deeper than any necromancer can plumb. The Underworld is a myth, and so is God. There shall be no coming back for you. And you will suffer before the end. Now, tell me: where is the pigment?"

Hao drew his eyes with aching slowness from the fire and fixed them upon Cali. Time stretched like the shadows lengthening as she began to summon her powers. The flame danced between them like a madwoman through the streets of some nameless city of eternal darkness. Hao sat: a toad, squat and motionless, his every atom a deadly toxin, his eyes never blinking or leaving her. Cali more resembled a terrible volcano, one about to erupt and blacken the skies with ash.

"Before the end..." Hao whispered, and perhaps it was the first time she had ever heard his voice stirred with passion. The intensity nearly stole her breath, and she found her resolve wavering, as though the eruption of lava might yet fail, collapsing inward, decimating the pinnacle of her selfhood. "Before the end, you will realise that the pigment was in your grasp—that you held it in your hands already—and you let it slip away."

"No," Cali hissed.

Hao smiled. Then he began to laugh.

"No," Cali said, now a roar. "No. Shut up, shut up, shut up!"

Hao moved with lightning speed, the leap of a toad traversing magical worlds, his gleaming form finally shedding all humanity, becoming a liquid whirlwind, a double-helix like the very strands of DNA that lived in all flesh, encoding meaning and existence in a language with no name. Twin serpents, entwined and forever revolving around one another but never meeting; emerald and purple, blue and red, white and black, diaphanous and dun. He was both and neither, a mere shedding, like a glittering robe discarded—yet flying toward her, opening, about to envelop her. The horror and wonder seized her at once. By the Black Star, where had he learned such magic? At the knee of Uboth? Hao was translucent and faceless and limbless, a butterfly's wing, a magic carpet sailing through the air, yet she knew with dream-certainty that the touch of his magical flesh would be—if not death—agony beyond measure. A jellyfish, then, seemingly listless and afloat, but poisonous and powerful when the tide carried it home.

Her consternation and surprise lasted only a moment, however. Power surged up through her throat as she gave a magical battlecry and raised the blade that had claimed the life of Alan Chambers. She did not swing the sword—such crude actions would not serve her against such a foe. Instead, she struck her own blade with her voice, set it to ringing, so that the hum reverberated in the dim chamber with the strength of a gong.

The translucent, jellyfish-like being paused, suspended by the force of the soundwaves. She knew the spell would not hold him long. Already he was changing. *Like water,* she thought. *Formless, utterly formless.* But she could not marvel at him, for then she would hesitate to deliver the killing blow. However much she longed to learn such magic, Hao would never teach her, and Uboth had long ago left the black planet in pursuit of his fanciful "Underworld". No, she must cast aside her greed and kill Hao now, kill him before he could ensnare her with his venomous arcana.

27

THE KING OF CARCOSA

"Hao!" she cried. "You once judged me unworthy. Now I pay you back in kind!"

There was a flash of light, a surge of flame. Her force was met by answering force; something serpentine and yet ethereal flashed and gyred; the walls were shaken by sounds deeper than the gulfs of Tartarus. Crown to foundation, Al Qaf Saba trembled.

And then, the flame was extinguished.

The light went out.

Cali stood alone in the darkness.

And the way lay open.

CHAPTER 6
DEPARTING URTH

THE TRIO SAT in the theatre that had once transported Alan to the black planet. Four flames burned, one in each corner, smoke disappearing into holes in the ceiling. A black and gold mat, woven with manalishi-worm thread, was spread across the floor, lending an erstwhile grandeur to the room.

"It's not working," LeBarron said. He had spent nearly a half hour supplicating the inner dreaming, but it did not answer his call. Whatever power had allowed him to transport Cassilda, Petruccio, and himself out of the court of Pe'kar seemed to have vanished. "I don't understand."

Cassilda noted LeBarron had lost some of the ethereal lustre that had cast him in the role of a shadowy warrior-god. Back in the dreaming desert, he'd seemed a being greater than a demon as he faced down Haercus, his sword ablaze, his body composed of smoke and darkness, his eyes terrifying jewels, crystallised only in the deathbed of worlds. But all that magic was gone now. She watched an actor fumbling with his lines, putting on airs, but without a shred of authenticity.

"It's because Alan is dead," Petruccio announced grimly.

Cassilda gritted her teeth. She hated how callously Petruccio spoke. She'd once admired that quality about him, but now, faced with a truth she could hardly accept, it seemed his deepest character-flaw.

"But it was *after* Cali struck that I did it," LeBarron said.

"Yes," the artist acknowledged. "But his spirit was still with the body, still *in the world*. Now, it's in some other place."

At this, LeBarron looked long and hard at Cassilda, as though wanting to reveal a secret, but too scared to follow through; she had no idea what it meant. She did, however, feel a well of emotion surge up, hot tears threatening to melt her icy composure. She remembered how Alan's corpse, though headless, had seemed to pitch itself backwards into the abyss, away from Cali's grasp. She had thought in that moment that, despite a mortal wound that should have killed him instantly, Alan had seemed to take action. Petruccio's hypothesis confirmed the idea, but there was little consolation in being proved right.

"Then what do we do?" LeBarron asked, sounding like a bewildered child.

"We do things the old-fashioned way," Petruccio said. "There are songs that may open doorways. It was how Cali brought her champions across. Cali was very practiced in this art, but I think the three of us together could pull it off."

"Music is magic," Cassilda muttered, remembering Alan and her singing together to escape the crumbling Temple of Namtar.

Again, the tears threatened. She hated such signs of weakness. Emotions and change had always been Cali's province. Cali rode the whirligig of life, the highs and lows, the moments of elation and the black pits of despair. Even as a girl, Cali had cleaved to the mountains and valleys of experience. But Cassilda had been even-tempered, never letting her formality and regality slip, save in the darkest and most intimate of moments. Now, it seemed, she had become like her sister, a creature ruled by her passions. *Albeit, my passions are of pain, not of pleasure, . . .* But was there really a difference? It was her pleasures, her hopes, her expectations that created such pain. Grief could only exist because she had known joy and love with Alan Chambers. *I should have shut myself away and never seen sun again!* She knew the thought to be false. It truly was better to have loved and lost.

"I will see if there are not some spare instruments for you and I," Petruccio said, speaking to LeBarron. His pragmatism was a welcome relief from her inner chaos. The actor nodded. The dwarf departed, but moments later returned carrying what looked to Cassilda like a crude form of ecg'tar (Petrucio explained it was a *sitar*, something earthlings had manufactured in imitation of Carcosa's instrument) and a tabla drum set.

Petruccio set the tabla down, then examined the room.

"We should form a triangle," he said. "After all, we are about to manifest something."

Cassilda raised her index finger, humming low beneath her breath. Her fingertip glowed, as though white hot. She set her finger upon the floor and its light scarred the carpet, burning a new pattern into its fabric that overlaid the old. She walked slowly, hunched over, tracing her glowing finger upon the cloth. Finally, she completed a near-perfect equilateral triangle.

LeBarron took up the sitar. He sat cross-legged at one corner of the triangle and strummed a few sweet chords. She hadn't known he could play, but it made sense. He'd travelled much of the black planet, performed in such a variety of dramas, it seemed logical he'd learned an instrument. She suspected he could sing too, though she doubted he knew how to infuse his song with magic.

Petruccio set up his tabla at the second corner of the triangle. It was an old and battered pair of drums; some of the dowels were broken and the hoops threadbare. She remembered Petruccio had carried a shiny new set with him when he and Cali first brought Alan to Carcosa. She wondered absently what had happened to it. Probably it was back at the palace.

The palace, that is where we must go, and swiftly. Cali would waste no time in bringing her full strength to bear. It was clear she could not be dissuaded from conquest and had a madman's absolute faith in victory.

Cassilda took her place at the third corner, completing the triangle. The triangle was ever a symbol connected with creation—and doorways. Was not the womb the doorway through which life entered the world? All things came into being through the womb. Even the universe itself was born from the void, which was another womb of a kind. Only one being had supposedly circumnavigated this primal law, and that was the God of whom her father had whispered—only in secret moments, rare occasions of vulnerability, in the sudden breaking of silences, or when awe and wonder had washed them in cleansing waters, witnessing some Carcosan miracle. He spoke of it with the hushed fervency of a conspiracy theorist, afraid that to speak too loudly is to invoke a cosmic wrath, or else to shatter the illusion entirely. At the time, she had thought her father's theological revelations to be nothing but eccentricity, for surely, *He* was a god? And it was difficult to

31

THE KING OF CARCOSA

imagine, especially as a child, anything more powerful than The King In Yellow. Only now did she see the truth. Her father had been speaking of deep things out of darkness, of what came before, for even He had a beginning. But there was *something* that had no beginning nor end. That thought terrified her to her deepest core.

"Cassilda . . . " She blinked and saw Petruccio, who was gently entreating her to return to the present.

"I'm sorry," she said. "Time is of the essence, I know."

Neither of them said anything, both understanding her pain and the maelstrom of her thoughts, for they shared in her fears.

"I think I know what song we must sing," she said. "Will you be able to follow?"

"Yes, dear princess," LeBarron said.

"Yes," Petruccio said.

Cassilda nodded in gratitude. She took a deep breath, centring herself. Her thoughts were still all-chaos, but with each breath, she drew herself further and further away from them, seeing them not as a part of her, but as ants crawling over a log, something busy and hivelike and curious, but ultimately small and of little consequence. The more she viewed her thoughts as separate, the more her mind—her true mind—quietened, and in that stillness, that void, potential began to brew.

It was in emptiness—the wastelands and the deserts—that energy manifested—like a pearl formed within the hollow pouch of a clamshell. Unlike her mind, she did not need to empty her heart, because it had already been bled of lifeblood, punctured like a gourd and drained of all vitality. *She* was empty, in mind, body, and soul. A vessel for imminence.

She raised her voice in song:

"Where is the maid, white as the moon
that I once loved in sable night?
Where is my heart, where joy's bright bloom?
She nevermore will see the light.

In Yhtill's marsh, I sought my rose,
but only monsters dwelt therein,
though no monsters could equal those
who squatted in my haunted mind.

32

In Hali's ice, I looked for her,
but found only the depths of sin.
I sought her in deep, dark Alar
but found my love had never been."

As she sang, a spirit began to fill up the room with the same asphyxiating closeness as choking smoke. Petruccio's textured rhythms kept her going, compelling her onward even though she felt like breaking down and crying. LeBarron's sitar notes were hesitant at first, a tinkling prelude, individual notes sparsely plucked, dying out as her voice climbed and climbed. But as the song went on, he gained confidence, his notes resonating, vibrating, morphing as they were heard into a form of onomatopoeic language. Rather than playing music, he seemed to be creating the soundscape of the song's story. She heard the roar of Yhtill's monsters, the cry of the wind, the footsteps of the lover seeking his love, even in the darkness and deepest of places. Her heart soared, and the sound that emerged from her was less music and more a tempest.

"The winds taught me the song of grief;
I followed them to Demhe's dreams,
but found only a false belief,
and nothing ever what it seemed.

Beyond Demhe, Pe'kar's domain,
the citadel of endless toil;
I sought her through those darkened lanes,
where hope—like virgin's cloth—is soiled."

Tears ran down her face, her hair blew in a breeze that should not exist. She was dimly aware of Petruccio and LeBarron exchanging glances, perhaps fear, perhaps wonderment. She closed her eyes so they would not distract her. The world trembled beneath her feet. She saw, with an inner eye, the vestiges of this reality falling away, like the clothes of the heir apparent stripped from the new king so that he may be reclothed in splendour. The emptiness in her heart had been filled with something else, with the joy of creation, with the magic of the ages. Even now, in the darkest despair, she could find that magic. And in it, she felt that Alan was no longer gone from her, that he was with her.

THE KING OF CARCOSA

"At last I found my love: she is
Nowhere, that place beyond the moon,
and suns, and even starlight's kiss:
and there her flower ever blooms!"

With those final words, a pulse ran through her, a quickening that was like an orgasm, though terrible, the death-throes of the organism, of the flesh-body, as though her spirit were an excretion to be expelled by its convulsions. She cried out. Petruccio and LeBarron likewise screamed. The whole universe shuddered as if with demonic pleasure.

She could not resist her temptation any longer. She opened her eyes and saw the gap between worlds. It was a sight her sister had beheld many times, but to Cassilda it was new. Blackness foamed and rushed about her. Stars hurtled through the dark, as though intent on celestial errands. Or was it *she* that was moving, streaking towards the far constellation of Taurus and the darkling glimmer of Aldebaran?

The spectacle reminded her of her father's secret room in the palace. Was that what it was, a place between worlds, forever in the liminal? And what would her father be searching for in such a place? Her questions fled as she beheld a new wonder—the dark was not merely the province of planets and stars. There were other forms here, forms that should not exist. With horror, she gasped. Things moving in the dark, eel-like and intelligent, large as planetary rings. Great cities rearing over gulfs that swallowed galaxies. Flowers, *flowers in the dark!*

Then she blinked and it was no more. She sat upon solid.stone, and before her was a vision that—had she been an ordinary mortal—would have driven her half-mad. To her, the hideous brightness of Carcosa was a welcome vision, as familiar as the freckles on a lover's face, as the nursery songs of childhood. The tears that flowed from her cheeks now were warm and comforting.

"Carcosa," she breathed. Never had a sight been gladder.

The tattered banners of the city flew in the whispering wind. The walls stood strong, though the gateway was still heavily damaged from when the Siege Ender had demolished it.

Petruccio and LeBarron sat a little way from her, both blinking, as though waking from a dream.

34

She was first to rise. The crumbling ruin around them was set upon a high rocky cliff overlooking the city. She was eager to make her way down, to warn the city of what was to come. But something held her a moment longer.

Impelled by a force beyond herself, some dark knowing—or perhaps it was even a connection with her sister, the bond of their blood inseparable even after so much pain—she turned and instead looked to the west, the direction of Demhe, and beyond: the lands of Blue Light. She knew it was madness to think she would see anything, but madness was indeed the ruling and ascendent sign of this age, for she *did* see something. Even her eyes, magically gifted, could not make out much in the way of detail, but the host was unmistakeable, larger than any the black planet had ever seen, making its way across the desert. The army resembled an ocean, dark as jet, creeping over the shoreline as the tide rushed in.

They did not have weeks to prepare the city for another siege and construct their weapon against Cali.

They had days.

Petruccio and LeBarron, noting her expression, got to their feet and tried to follow her gaze, but their eyes struggled.

"Is it Cali?" Petruccio said.

"Yes," Cassilda said. "She has made frightening progress. Or else we have lost time."

"Then we should waste no more of it." LeBarron clutched *Hope Reborn*. His bewilderment had left, replaced with a hardened resolve that seemed only a little feigned.

He may not have the gift of the pigment, Cassilda thought, *but that sword could end even Cali should he manage to strike her.*

Perhaps, after all, some good would come from Pe'kar's creations.

"I'll show you the way down," Petruccio said.

He led them to the path that wound down the side of the rockface, and then across the sands, towards the ruined gateway of Dim Carcosa.

Storm clouds gathered overhead.

CHAPTER 7
ANDREW

ABRACADABRA SEARCHED THE garden but could not find The King. He began to grow concerned. Night was upon him, and though the garden had hitherto felt safe, it was also full of things he did not understand: strange creatures, mysterious flowers, places where time and reality did not seem to obey the laws he knew. Death was an illusion, so The King had said, but death was not the only possibility in a place that seemingly had no horizon.

He wandered for what felt like a lifetime, discovering more hidden pearls of the nameless garden. There were glades where sound died away, leaving a silence so absolute he wept; dells glittered with lights that seemed the lights of a far-off city, and indeed they were, metropoli no larger than a dinner plate sprawled across the boughs of intertwined trees, bustling with microcosmic activity. He longed to explore these miniature worlds, but he had to go on. The garden was leading him somewhere, with the subtlest of suggestions: shrubs and thickets parting to reveal new paths, starlight dancing into the gaps between trees where previously he might not have looked, warm winds—carrying the sweetest aromas—nudging him like an autumnal leaf on his wayward path.

The birdsong of the garden had changed with the coming of night. Owls hooted, their eyes glinting in the treetops. Blackbirds conversed in melodic languages. Nightingales sang as if in mourning for the banished sun. *Was it sun singular or plural?* Abracadabra wondered. While walking the day-lit garden he hadn't paid attention. Now he was curious whether the garden shared this strange feature of the black planet, though the memories of that former life seemed as much a haze the inchoate forms swooping to and fro in the dark.

At last, he came to a strangeness that brought him short, something profoundly out of place in the wonders of the garden. It was a structure that could only have been manmade, though primitive.

A circle had been formed from upright staves. The staves had been stripped of errant branches, though they were far from smooth. They had been driven deep into the ground and formed a ring roughly five-feet high. In the gaps between these staves, Abracadabra could see a figure crouched over. He heard the figure too, a muttering sound, very guttural, all vowels that seemed to have been dug up from the earth.

Slowly, Abracadabra circled the magical ring, never taking his eyes off the figure in its centre. He came to a place where there was an opening in the staves. No sooner did he align with this doorway than the figure in the middle of the circle looked up sharply. Abracadabra was immediately struck by the man—for it was a man—and the sheer intensity of his gaze. The eyes seemed to reach out of their sockets and pierce him like dagger-blades. His features were Edwardian, sharp, austere, as though their owner brooked no foolishness nor argument. He was moon-pale, and gifted with black, lustrous hair. His beard had been styled into a Machiavellian goatee, which was the only evidence of humour, a self-awareness of his own pretensions and the performative nature of reality.

The man slowly straightened. He was tall and wore black monk-like robes, stretched by a slight paunch, bound with a cingulum. He could have been a Catholic priest save for the design on the chest of his robe was not a Christian symbol.

"Who are you?" Abracadabra asked, with the same directness and fascination as a child.

"My name is Andrew, though some call me Alogos . . . As to who I am, well, I am *you*. Or rather, I could have been."

Abracadabra frowned.

"You are a magician?"

Andrew smiled.

"No, though it is an easy mistake to make. I am a mystic."

"What's the difference?"

A shadow passed across Andrew's face. The glimmering eyes burned like volcanic depths.

THE KING OF CARCOSA

"A magician returns from beyond the threshold. The mystic remains. Come, enter my circle, sit a while. We have much to discuss."

It was only once Abracadabra had stepped past the doorway and into the circle that he questioned whether he should have, whether he was putting himself in some mortal danger. But Andrew made no move. He sat down cross-legged and motioned for his new guest to do the same.

Sitting, Abracadabra pondered a question to ask, but before he could, Andrew spoke.

"What do you know about consciousness?"

Abracadabra was taken aback.

"What do you mean?"

Andrew remained impassive.

"What do you know?"

"I know that I am pure awareness, pure being," Abracadabra said. "The observer and not the doer."

Andrew frowned. The harshness such an expression gifted his face was like the serrated edge of a saw.

"That is something you memorised from a textbook. Or something someone else told you. Do you think that you can win this war with the intellect alone?"

"War?" The notion seemed absurd in the midst of the ever flowering garden of secrets.

Andrew nodded slowly.

"Yes, war. This is the realm of spirit. But the spirit and flesh are one. What we do here echoes there and vice-versa. This is because the universe is made from the cloth of the Self. You look at the universe and think of it as other, but in truth, it is made from your own flesh. What you perceive is yourself in the darkling mirror, the illusion we call 'life'. To know this is wisdom, but to *use* it is magic." Andrew let out a sudden bark of frustration, something between a cough and a dog's angry shout. He gritted his teeth, muttered something unintelligible under his breath. "If you are here, it means you failed as I did, Alan Chambers."

Every hair upon Abracadabra's arms and neck stood on end. His breath caught in his throat. As it did so, it seemed the garden shimmered, as though what he perceived as solid reality was in fact an image projected onto water, and the water was beginning to undulate with the coming of a wave.

"Yes, that was your name once—and the name of a star is its light given voice. But it is a false name, just as 'Andrew' is a false name. We are more alike than you could know. Both of us were claimed by the eidolon of our obsession."

"Cali . . . " Abracadabra whispered.

The name seemed to cause the garden to dim, the stars winking out, and dark things to edge from the shadows of trees and listen to their words

"Yes, Cali," Andrew said. "But unlike me, *you* have the option of returning, of facing her one final time."

"Then *let* me return!" Abracadabra said. "The King said I must do so. And I want to. Let me face her."

Andrew shook his head.

"You are not ready yet. But it is our role to make sure that you are."

"Our? There are others?"

"Yes, most certainly. More names than can be counted walk the paths of this garden. But you will meet three, of which I am the first."

"The ghost of Christmas past, present, and future?" Abracadabra said, though for a moment he was not Abracadabra, he was Alan Chambers again, and a small gladness overtook him, like a ray of sun piercing the clouds.

Andrew bequeathed him with the subtlest of smiles.

"Perhaps. Though whether I am your past, present, or future is not clear. Perhaps it would be better to think of it in terms of three states of being."

Abracadabra frowned.

Andrew raised his hand and counted off three fingers

"Waking, dreaming, sleeping. Or, conscious, dreaming, and unconscious. I am your unconscious self, the mastery and power than lies dormant and sleeping within you. I could have been ten times the magician you are, but Cali stopped me. Cut was the branch that might have grown strong . . . "

Abracadabra sensed no ego in Andrew's words—this was not vain boasting—only a dreadful certainty, hard as diamond. He experienced a sudden longing to have met Andrew in the living world, to have witnessed his power, to have learned from him over long years. Still, he should be grateful for even this moment of illumination.

THE KING OF CARCOSA

"How do I access this power?" Abracadabra whispered.

Andrew smiled.

"You want to know? It is simple: *seize it now!*" Suddenly he leapt forward, his legs uncrossing to propel him through the air like a frog. His agility was surprising given his weight and posture. The palm of Andrew's hand struck Abracadabra's forehead with stultifying force, and a cry left Abracadabra's lips, at once wracked with terrible pain but also orgasmic, a release, as though a knot in his brain had been suddenly undone. Colours swam before his vision, chirals and coils of maddening complexity. He felt as though he were tumbling backward, the colours rising up around him from some deep fissure below. He searched for a pattern, a logic to be found, but at first it was opaque to him. Colours flashed, processed, swirled, coalesced, undulated, then vanished. He was at once part of the colours, encoiled by them, but also totally separate, a disembodied observer with less agency than a ghost.

The moment seemed to last an age, but time shifted into forward gear again as he realised that he was looking at *scales,* a great cosmic serpent of transcendental beauty. He glimpsed it in fullness only a moment, the way its skin formed an iridescence as of a thousand rainbows, and then it was gone. He stared up at the night sky, empty save for the pinpricks of faraway planets and stars. Sitting slowly upright—for he had fallen backward—he found the circle to be empty, and Andrew Alogos gone.

CHAPTER 8
THE LAST OF THE SERPENTKIN

C ALI STARED DOWN at Al Shujah. The backwater little town had been spared by Pe'kar on his long march to Carcosa, but she would not be so merciful.

Once, Al Shujah had been clad in the glamour of dreaming, a beggar dressed in the bejewelled robes of a king. But now, robbed of such evasive splendours, which had courted the realms of impossible beauties and nightmarish horrors, it seemed nothing more than a filthy grotto, a bowl filled with the excrement and dust of dying men.

She could not hold back her army anymore. She had to let them have some fun . . .

"Burn it to the ground!" she said.

Malebolge the Cruel, who hovered at her side, grinned. His face was too little flesh stretched over too much bone, including what must have been five hundred needle teeth. He spread his wings and took flight, relaying her orders to the others. Within moments, the gorgonopsid calvary surged forward, readying the line for a spearhead. Such force was utterly unnecessary, but it would make for a potent demonstration, and give the army something to expend their pent-up energies upon. She had denied them the opportunity at Al Qaf Saba, preferring to take all the pleasure herself . . .

Deep, deep she had delved into the heart of the mountain. At the end of the impossibly long passageway, spiralling down into the foundations of the black planet, she had once again beheld the Temple of the Serpentkin, with its obscene ostentation, its gilded arrogance. Every curlicued spire and colonnade was an affront to the magic Cali wielded, to the journey she had been forced to

41

undertake, to the lashes and scars she bore. The gleaming yellow marks on her body still reminded her, daily, of Alan Chambers and the power of The Claw. They reminded her of how she—of all people—had been deemed unworthy in their eyes to take the pigment.

She had punished them for that, bathing in their blood and drinking their power.

After killing all but one serpentkin, an ageing nagini, Cali gave her the false hope of a swift death if she revealed where the pigment was.

The nagini had spat in her face, and Cali had performed excruciations upon her worthy of Pe'kar.

When all that was left were twitching parts, kept alive by a cursed form of magic, Cali had finally realised that the nagini either did not know the location, or had been so brainwashed as to be impossible to break. She had devoured her while the last throbbing life still pulsed in her dismembered body.

Cali licked her lips with pleasure at the memory. Poets said revenge never satisfied, that it left bitterness in the mouth, but all she could taste was the sweetness of their despair. *What do poets know?* She thought of the fool LeBarron, and of Petruccio her old servant—they were so wrapped up in their creations that they could not seize reality. It passed them by, like liquid gold running through their fingertips, while they tried to grasp abstractions. Once, Cali had styled herself as a philosopher—she remembered all too well her lengthy conversations with Alan in the marshes, educating him on some improbable theorem of reality—but now she saw the pure, moronic vanity of it. It was pointless to contemplate the world's creation, pointless to contemplate her father's riddles, pointless to imagine new dreams—there was only the here and now, the moment to be seized in a bloody hand. That was why she would win. Her new outlook had already served her against the serpentkin—their dusty, academic preponderances had protected them naught. O, how delicious it had been when they had, as one, raised their spells against her—and found them wanting! Cali's answering spell cracked the great temple, brought it crumbling upon their heads. She could have shattered the mountain if she'd wished. But she decided it would be better to leave it there as a tombstone, a monument that celebrated the absolute triumph of the Demon Queen over all who opposed.

"With me! On my command!" Cali raised her sword in the air, kicking Satan's flanks, though she needn't have done so: the cunning gorgonopsid had anticipated her will and was already galloping forward, the thunder of his footfalls more riotous than a storm.

Guards stood at the gate, but with a single magical cry they were shorn of their armour and then flesh, falling from their posts like savaged birds, tattered rags of skin blown on the winds of change.

I should make a human skin-suit my banner, she thought. *That will strike terror into the heart of Carcosa.*

Through the gate she stormed. Clusters of villagers turned in surprise, their faces contorting with horror. A kick of Satan's flanks and he was upon them, crushing a male villager with disgusting weight. The gorgonopsid sank jaws into the man's throat and tore with a catlike hiss.

Cali's sword flashed and a woman fell headless to the ground.

Calian cavalry flooded in behind her, their faces alight with savage glee, their swords shining with Pe'kar's bile (for great quantities had been stored up over the centuries, enough to last until the end of this war at least), their steeds as hungry as their masters.

Her blood was up, like a madman beneath the moon's dreadful influences, the tides of her soul dragged towards calamitous violence. Satan relinquished the corpse of his prey and pounced upon another fleeing villager. The gorgonopsid's forepaws broke the villager's spine instantly. They lay mewling and pinned beneath the draconian creature as it took a bite out of the back of their skull, a gush of crimson spilling from the brainpan like a libation to a new, dark goddess. Two more villagers ran beyond the reach of Cali's sword. She sheathed it, though still bloody, and then drew up her harp, which was affixed to her belt via an iron chain. One strum of the harp's grizzly strings and a jangle of dissonant sound ossified in the air, as though she might conjure shapes from prehistory, breathe life into the fixed clay of fossils. But it was not life she brought, only death. A second strum set the phantasmal solidity in motion, like a comet, or a boulder hurled by a giant. The discordance shrieked as it passed through air. The vengeful spirit smashed into the spines of the fleeing villagers and ripped them asunder, their limbs torn out of their sockets, their ribcages burst open, exposing the hollow chambers that housed their still-beating hearts. They died screaming, mutilated beyond recognition.

Cavalry surged around Cali, gorgonopsids feasting upon the fallen, tearing into the legs of those still standing, bringing them down. Spears flashed in the sun, impaling helpless farmers and merchants. Costermonger stalls were overturned, like flapping thin-boned creatures, their coloured cloths dyed a new red; fruits, bread, and other homely delicacies were crushed beneath the trample of clawed feet; phials and phylacteries were cast to the ground and broken, their esoteric contents spilling, consumed by greedy sand. Guards came to defend the village, but they were ill-equipped in all senses, most not having seen combat in decades. The Calians, hungry for bloodlust, ensorcelled by the glory of their new queen, butchered them with the ease of one hacking apart a lifeless slab of meat.

From the skies, trueborns descended, lifting up villagers like eagles snatching up defenceless creatures of the dirt.

Cali had commanded the experimental horrors to be held back. She would only use them against the walls of Carcosa itself.

She drove farther into the village. She sensed there was something here for her to find, though she knew not what. A woman ran across her path squealing in terror; she was naked and covered head to toe in blood. A red woman . . .

The vision startled her, pulled her out of the moment and into another place and time.

A name rose to her lips.

"Babylon."

It had been a long time since she played the role of Red Goddess. But before Andrew and Austin, there had been Aleister. Poor, tormented, fecund, frightened Aleister, acting out the role of both master and slave with equal vigour, torn between two polarities that eventually would rip him asunder. He could well have been her champion—he had the power and intuition, combined with one other factor so many men lacked: receptivity.

She had painted herself red for him, portrayed herself as Babylon, his great goddess of bloodshed and Truth, ravaged his mind with a vision worthy of St. John.

He had become a powerful magician. Some would argue the most powerful of all the champions she had corralled and seduced. But in the end, magic had used him up. Magic had been another drug to Aleister, another method of deranging the senses and accessing altered states. This abusive of power could not go unpunished. In the end, Cali had not needed to lift a finger to destroy Aleister: he had destroyed himself, dying alone and bedridden, feeble where once he had been all-conquering, doubtful where he had once shaped nations to his will. If he had been able to free himself from his addictions, he might have proved very useful indeed to Cali. But he would not be the first soul who, having ventured to the shores of Carcosa's madness, had found solace in the reprieve of chemical substances.

"Cali!"

The voice called her back to reality, to the present moment. Her first thought was that it was one of her lieutenants, but the voice was not one of appeal, but a challenge.

She searched and soon found its source: a pale naga-woman occupied the centre of one street. Where all else was panic, chaos, and bloodshed, she stood as a flawless diamond, immune to the stain of fear. The white skin of her upper body was a dazzling cloth of starlight, cloaking her inner being, which shone forth with a radiance visible only to those with magical sight. Her dark hair flew in the breeze like seaweed in the ocean's depths. There was something altogether aquatic about her: the eel-like, sinuous coils of her snake-tail, the brightness of her eyes like something that lived in the sunless deeps. She bore no weapon, but Cali knew that the woman carried magic within her.

"Who are you, then?" Cali said, pulling on Satan's reins to slow his approach. The beast was muzzled in gore, licking his lips, his eyes cocaine-wide and burning with even greater Desire than his master. "And what is one of your kind doing here, in this backwater town?" Cali smiled darkly. "Should you not have died with your brothers and sisters in what was once Al Qaf Saba?"

"I am Liliya," the nagini said. Her eyes closed with religious solemnity. "And it was not my destiny to die with my brothers and sisters. It was my destiny to meet you here."

Cali sneered.

"You think, with all the foes I have faced, all the obstacles overcome, with an army at my back . . . You think *you* will be the one to stop me?"

Liliya opened her eyes and smiled.

"I did not say that. But I doubt very much you will set your dogs

45

of war upon me. A part of you still cleaves to the old ways, to a warrior's tradition, however much you wish to deny it. You want to face me in single combat, magician against magician, and prove you're the best."

Cali smiled, though it was a forced rictus. The slaughter continued around her, though some soldiers were gathering to her side, perceiving a new threat, anxious to be given orders.

But the nagini was right. Cali would not send lackeys to do her work, nor pass up the opportunity to exorcise her new strength against a worthier foe. She wanted to break this Liliya, just as she had broken the rest of her kind.

Slowly, Cali dismounted from Satan. The beast growled, but she hushed it with a single hand upon its brow. Submitting to the will of his master, he paced to one side, chewing the flesh of a corpse to content himself in the meantime.

Cali faced Liliya.

"I killed them all, you know," Cali said with relish. "Those who dwelt beneath the mountain. They set themselves upon a throne as the paragons of knowledge and wisdom, yet they knew nothing. I swept away all traces of them—all memory of their culture—in a single day. I gave them terror. Many of them begged me for death. Their pride was easy to break, in the end. I wonder if you will be the same, proud Liliya?"

"Indeed?" Liliya said, with a cold detachment that was as infuriating as it was admirable. "But it seems for all their terror they did not reveal to you the secret of the pigment."

Cali felt a shadow pass across the waters of her soul. Then a fire kindled, like some volcanic fissure opening in a deep grave of the sea.

Liliya smiled.

"Is that why you came here with sword drawn? A little temper tantrum, having been denied the one thing that can save you from him."

"Him?" Cali snarled. There was only one person she could mean. "Alan Chambers is dead, you whore. I cut off his head. He is nothing!"

And still Liliya defied her with that implacable smile.

"Of course Alan Chambers is dead. But that was never his true name or nature. You know that as well as I."

Cali felt rage building inside her, a Vesuvius of hatred for this arrogant witch stood in her path.

"What would you know of his name or nature?" Cali snarled. "It was I who slew him!"

"And it was I who gave birth to him. I laid the egg, fertile with the seed of man, that became the serpent-born hero of Truth."

Cali almost staggered. The force of those words was like a vacuum, sucking the atmosphere away, leaving her as a ship marooned upon a windless sea, mad and craven and cursed. She could offer no reply, no rebuttal. Shame, jealousy, wrath, all burned within her like a pit of vipers striking at one another. At the same time, she struggled to reclaim thought or agency, a doomed vessel abandoned by elements and God.

"You . . . you are his mother?"

"Yes. And it was I, not Uboth, who chose his secret name. And I alone who know its true meaning."

"The meaning is irrelevant," Cali snarled, desperately trying to recover herself. "He is dead.

"If that is what you choose to believe, then so be it," Liliya replied, her smile a crimson radiance that daunted even Cali's tigress-heart. "But I think we both know that it is never fatal when a serpent sheds its skin."

Cali screamed.

In an instant, both unleashed their magic. Cali's power was like a tsunami, an elemental force released from the prison of a dam: unrestrained, virtually undirected, sweeping towards her foe with a fury that was as mindless as it was deadly. Buildings either side were ruptured by its passage; the ground cracked. Overhead, carrion birds died, where they thought they had flown safely above the massacre. Earth, sand, and stone were ripped from their moorings and carried along with the wave of magical force.

Liliya's answer was its exact opposite. A shield arose, a force as sculpted as a Michaelangelo, indomitable as granite. Cali's wave met this force, and the crack was a thunder the world had never known. Colours speared in every direction like light shot through a prism. Where these colours touched, transformations took place. Corpses gave birth to flowering trees. Buildings were levelled, and their rubble formed swirling wells of stone, as though even solid matter could be turned into quicksand. Sand became a carpet of priceless pearl, glittering in the sun.

Liliya almost collapsed forward, her breath ragged. It had taken every last ounce of magical strength to repel the first blast.

THE KING OF CARCOSA

Cali had not even begun her assault in earnest. She drew up her harp, and her fingers began to dance across the strings. The instrument was far cruder and more limited than her twenty-two stringed ecg'tar, but what it lacked in subtlety and complexity, it made up for in purity of power.

The notes resonated with the fullness of an ancient gong. Each one reverberated at a level deeper even than sound—at the level of spirit. The ancient Indian gurus had called this the "subtle body", an energy that permeated everything. Cali was done using the subtle energy of the world to influence the material one, however. That seemed cumbersome, the province of petty conjurers, of little-minded magicians. She was a god, not a sorcerer. She was going to reach directly into the subtle, etheric realm and destroy the soul of her enemy where it resided.

The melody began slowly, each note hanging in the air like a guillotine blade. Liliya raised her voice in song, a counterspell, but it was drowned beneath the thunder of the harp.

"This instrument was carved from one of the Two Trees," Cali said. "And its strings were harvested from the flesh of a trueborn son of Pe'kar. You have no power that can resist it. You will dance for me as a puppet would."

Cali struck a note, a certain jarring cluster of resonances, not truly a chord—for a chord suggested harmony—more a word spelled in a language hateful to all divinities, a language God had tried to erase with the great flood of biblical legend.

Liliya screamed, no longer able to resist the word of power. Her limbs were seized by a force as invisible as it was terrifying, and she began to float upward, drawn by an unseen hand. Her tail thrashed upon the ground, but it could not move her. She was being pulled skyward from the crown of her head as if by a single but unbreakable thread.

Cali laughed, but her fingers never ceased their dance. Though Cali acted, she felt like the one acted upon, as though a spirit played through her, teaching her the secret meanings of this new language. With her ecg'tar, she had done impossible things, but she knew all those powers were nothing compared to what she would accomplish with the harp.

I shall level Carcosa and raise it up anew. I shall drown my enemies in a sea of blood and build an island upon it. A thousand skulls shall be my throne! I am the Black Empress!

It seemed as though new strings were being attached to Liliya, her arms stretched out one by one, until she was cruciform, a shuddering power exerting itself upon her body, pulling at every joint, intent to un-seam her. Cali could see rips appearing in her flesh as the limbs were twisted out of place. The cracking of bones accompanied the insane rhythms of the eldritch harp.

"If truly you are the mother of Alan Chambers," Cali said. "Then you should thank me, witch: for soon you shall be with your son!"

For a moment, it seemed Liliya would die wordlessly, the agony of her torment too much. But then, a smile split her features.

"We shall all be with him," she said. "Save you! You shall be Nothing!"

Then Liliya's head was wrenched from her torso. Blood fountained. Cali's fingers halted, though the music of the instrument seemed to live on, as though bouncing off the walls of reality itself, echoing back to her, evidence of some terrible emptiness that lived at the heart of existence. Liliya's headless corpse fell to the floor. The head bounced and rolled like a football—such was the stupid comedy of mortal lives.

She died like her son, Cali thought. *Though this time, the blood shall be mine.*

The building Liliya had defended was aptly named *The Bloody Graal*; aptly, because Cali had just drained her corpse of all its blood, leaving the withered flesh like an empty water-skin upon the sand, to be torn by gorgonopsids.

She did not know why she felt drawn to this place, but she had decided to enter. The tavern seemed deserted. Empty tables and stools stood like tombstones in a graveyard. A long bar, with a multitude of barrels and glass bottles behind it, was the only evidence *The Bloody Graal* had once been a busy tavern. Crimson banners hung from the walls. The ebony woodwork was surprisingly ornate, baroque even, for an establishment that dwelt in the middle of a dustbowl.

A large stairwell descended into the main room. She mounted it and ascended to the first floor. A corridor with a series of rooms presented itself. Now she knew why she had come here, for she could hear breathing a few doors down. Someone was here. Cali would find out who.

She did not bother silencing her steps or preparing any cantrips. She was the Demon Queen, and undoubtedly the greatest threat in Al Shujah lay dead outside. Cali had made herself even stronger with Liliya's blood—though the exercise seemed pointless at this stage.

The Demon Queen pushed open the door and was taken aback. Of all the things she had expected, she had not foreseen a room full of frightened little children. They stared at her with horror and awe. What must she look like to them? Covered in blood? Bearing the eyes of a snake but the body of a goddess? Children, also, could always smell magic. Cali must reek of it.

"You're not Mother Liliya," a little girl said.

Cali searched their faces.

"What was Liliya doing to you?" Her darkest suspicions had been evoked.

"She gave us a warm bath."

"She helped us," another said. "We were so thirsty after walking through the desert."

"The demons put us in chains," a brave boy piped up. "But Princess Cassilda set us free!"

"She's the greatest magician in the whole world!" the first girl agreed, enthusiastically.

Cali felt her lip curl involuntarily, her snarl ten times more ferocious and terrifying than that of the gorgonopsid who so often was at her side.

"Satan . . . " she whispered.

The beast had followed her into *The Blood Graal,* silent as Death himself. He padded forward, mouth open, drool flecking its teeth.

All children were fascinated by animals, but they also feared their unpredictability.

"Who is the greatest magician in the world?" Cali said. Her eyelid twitched. She felt outside of herself, watching some avatar or mummer enact her life, while she powerlessly observed.

They are only children, she thought. *They can be forgiven their ignorance.* But yet here was another way her sister had cheated her, *denied* her. The Black Empress stood before them, yet these dirty, stupid children praised her sister.

Let it go, a voice implored.

But who was Cali to listen? She was the god of the black planet. *I decide what is right!*

And there was no room for dissension. There must be thirty children here. All of them would grow up with the memory of Cassilda as their saviour, and once Cali disposed of her sister, they would naturally ally themselves against Cali, either individually or as a group. Here was a breeding ground for rebellion. They were no threat now, but each one could grow up to become another Alan Chambers, another thorn in her side.

"Where is Mother Liliya?" the brave little boy asked.

Cali turned away. It was the first time in long eons she had averted her eyes to anything.

"Mother isn't coming home."

She made a clicking noise at the back of her throat; the gorgonopsid obeyed the will of his master.

The screams followed Cali out of the door as she left Satan to his feast.

CHAPTER 9
THE VAULTS

C ASSILDA WAS RECEIVED back into the city to cries of jubilation. The sentries, nobles, and townsfolk raised their voices in joyful proclamations. *The Princess of Carcosa returns!* Though she had never been popular, the death of Hastur had left a vacuum, a vacuum which had only become more pronounced when Cassilda and the others set off in pursuit of Cali. Glad though she was to lift spirits with her return, she cut all celebration short.

"We must prepare for battle," she commanded. "At once."

The captain of the guard, chosen to command in Roland's stead while he journeyed to the lands of Blue Light, was a warrior called Abratax. He was of similar build to Roland, though squatter and broader, and his skin was a sun-kissed mahogany rather than a jetstone black. He had styled his eurypterid helmet with a quinel-hair plume. The Yellow Sign blazed proudly upon his cheek. He bowed low to Cassilda.

"If I may be permitted a question, your highness?"

"You may."

"What of Roland?"

Her heart felt as though it had been clad in ugly pig-iron.

"I am sorry, Abratax. Roland perished in battle, though he slew many of Pe'kar's soldiers." *Not Pe'kar's, anymore. They belong to Cali, as does the army heading our way.* "There is much we must apprise you and the courtiers of."

The Carcosan soldiers did not tarry after that, but rushed to obey, relaying orders and messages to key officials, marshalling a squadron to accompany the trio to the palace, and informing Cassilda of what had taken place during her absence.

As they walked from the gate to the palace, a gloaming covered the city in shadow, the twin suns setting. Cassilda tried not to read symbolic meaning in the dying of the light.

When they were finally secluded in a discreet room of the palace, Abratax—armed with many missives and notes from the various factions within the city—gave them all they needed to know. But with all the updates on the ludicrously complex politics of Carcosa, the jostling of courtiers for power, the actions of the priesthoods, and the movements of the cannibals, Cassilda realised there was one piece missing.

"What of the children?"

"I'm sorry, your highness?" Abratax looked perplexed.

"The children. We freed a group of children in the lands of Blue Light. I created a nagual to guide them back here . . . Have they not arrived?"

Abratax's face shadowed.

"If they have, none of my watchmen received them."

Cassilda hung her head in grief. A curse left her lips that seemed to carry with it the fellest winds of the black planet, winds blowing out of the void of despair. Even after the violations of The Stranger, Cassilda had not known despair like this. She had known shame, ignominy, and terrible, terrible pain. But always she had believed in the purposeful nature of her life, that she must keep going forward. Alan's death, however, had opened a door onto an abyss that previously she could not have believed existed. And it seemed no matter what she did she could not close such a door. She had to live, for the rest of her life, with one eye forever on the darkness lying beyond that door, troubled by the spirits of hell that rose from its bottomless depths to plague her with rancid doubts and blackest depressions. *The wound is still fresh. Give it time,* she thought. But she knew such rationalisations were powerless against her true feeling, which was that there was little point now in what they did. The battle was already lost. The victory of her sister assured. They were mere puppets going through motions ordained by cosmic ordinances.

"You did all you could," LeBarron said.

"Spare me your cliches," she snarled. A sigh left her lips. "I'm sorry, LeBarron."

"No, you are right. Such sentiments are inadequate."

"We do not know they are dead," Petruccio said. "We must retain our grip upon reality, upon absolute facts."

THE KING OF CARCOSA

"Such things do not exist," Cassilda said. "Not in this world."

"No," Petruccio admitted. "Nor upon Earth, either. All truth is relative, and all facts interpreted . . . *However,* there are greater and lesser certainties. We do not know if the children were apprehended. They may be simply slow in returning. For now, we face greater problems. Cali is upon us."

Abratax looked grave, though there was also a resolution in his eyes that strengthened Cassilda's waning will. There were soldiers here still ready to fight, who needed someone to lead them, and frankly there was no one left save her.

"How are the garrisons, Captain Abratax?"

"Not as replenished as we might have hoped, but since the . . . the dead ones fell away, we have rebuilt our numbers to a few thousand strong."

The trio exchanged dark glances.

"We know what we're up against," Abratax said. "The army is visible to the naked eye now. By my estimation, a hundred thousand at least." The soldier looked at them each in turn, bravely meeting their eyes as he delivered the grim news. "Naturally, panic is spreading through the city. Rumours, too. They say Cali has become a god, among other things. The people are not ready for another siege. Not with the loss of the King—*Hideous and Bright is He.*" The praise sounded hollow and lifeless, a mere formality. Cassilda mourned. Once, every soldier in Carcosa had bellowed the words with the vitality of a skylark. "If I may, your highness, we need the Claw-bearer. Many witnessed his defence of the King—*Glorious His Deeds*—and saw him defeat the Siege Ender. If he were to make an appearance publicly, perhaps deliver a speech written by your mummer companion, then it would surely raise spirits, rally the soldiers and civilians alike."

Cassilda turned away. She could not face Abratax with tears.

Petruccio cleared his throat. "The Claw-bearer fell."

A stunned silence greeted this pronouncement.

"And . . . And The Claw itself?"

"In the hands of the enemy," LeBarron said, solemnly.

"Your tidings are graver and graver," Abratax said. "Never has Carcosa known a darker hour..."

Cassilda could not speak. She could not do anything. She felt as though she had been paralysed by a spider's venom, wrapped in its web, waiting in helpless agony as its poisons turned her insides into liquid food for the arachnid's hungry maw. Petruccio, however, held the line.

"Captain, I know the despair that lives in your eyes, for the spectre is with us also. But there is still hope. We must be given access to the vaults, at once."

Abratax frowned.

"Only the Head Courtier can authorise such access."

For a moment, there was only silence. Then Petruccio began to laugh—a mad laugh, like a clown at the end of the world. Such was the strange, razor-edge of his hilarity that Cassilda soon found herself laughing with him. LeBarron followed suit. And then even the stern, tight-lipped captain was chuckling, though he knew not at what. Their laughter flowed out of the secret palace room, through its echoing hallways, past the gossiping courtiers, down the steps, and into the fluid streets of the insane citadel. The church bells began to peal in unison, joining in with the laughter too.

It was a terrible laughter, the laughter of a suicidal gunman whose last bullet has jammed in the chamber, the laughter of gods indwelling the primordial night, perceiving the desperation with which mortals cling to life.

But it was not only laughter. The churches also gave warning. For the great, living, organistic buildings perceived the dark tide that marched upon the city.

Cali was almost at their doorstep.

Once the defensive preparation had been set in motion, with Abratax given detailed instructions to be relayed to every commanding officer in the Carcosan army, the trio wasted no further time. Petruccio had little difficulty obtaining a key for the vaults, though it was clear the courtiers had thought the dwarf was never coming back, ceding his authority long ago to one of their own, a purple-robed savant by the name of Geb. Geb, despite the disgruntlement of the other courtiers, graciously bequeathed the key to Petruccio, performing all the formalities with unctuous enthusiasm. Petruccio thought that in all likelihood Geb was glad to pass the burden of responsibility, especially in the light of imminent crisis. That, and Petruccio's shadow stretched longer than it had any right to. Men three times his height felt diminished by his presence.

The vaults could only be reached by passing through three magical doorways, each one grouchier than the last (though none quite so obstinate as Hephaiton). The final door lay at the bottom of a stairwell that ran down deep into the palace's foundations, deeper even than the prison cells and the Screaming Pit. Cassilda had explored these same corridors as a little girl, along with her sister, following rumours of ancient beasts and giant coprophages who dwelt in the secret passages. Of course, her sister had always been the one scolded for wandering . . .

Now, descending the slippery, onyx stairs, she wondered how she had ever found the courage to explore this place—it sent shivers down her spine.

Cassilda led the way, humming a soft note that caused light to shine from her skin. Petruccio came next. LeBarron walked at their rear. The mummer, of all of them, seemed most afraid—or perhaps he was simply anxious with excitement. She found it strange that one who had gone beyond death more than once could fear anything. Then again, it depended what waited on the other side. Her father had spoken of paradisal gardens for those who believed in the True Magic—but that left the question of what waited for those who did not.

Somewhere not dissimilar from this stairwell, she thought. *A dark descent, slippery and without footing, blind and rotten and precipitous, a blackness below ever yawning, and shadows upon the walls.*

Deeper and deeper they went. The strangest thing of all was the stairs had no turns. It plummeted straight down, at a horribly steep angle, its walls unadorned save for the grooves of colossal stone slabs, the stairs themselves rough-hewn and strangely slippery. It was cold here, yet moist, as though the lower levels had been flooded by stagnant water. Cassilda couldn't remember if it had always been this way. In Carcosa, rot was not treated the same way as on Earth. Decay was a living thing, a growing mycelial lifeform, and who knew what new things might spring from its fecundity.

After a while—what may have been halfway, though Cassilda was struggling to remember, her recollections of childhood distorted by the intense emotions of youth—Cassilda paused.

"Erik would have come this way," she said, mournfully. "It was once his duty to manage the vaults, to keep their secrets safe."

"Would that he had not hidden such secrets from Cali," Petruccio said, darkly.

Cassilda nodded.

"She already knew the secrets of what lay down here, better than me. Erik was merely the one to fetch materials for her, to make her plans seem legitimate. If he'd refused, I doubt it would have delayed her long. She would have found another way."

They continued in stony silence, and after what felt like hours, the stairwell finally ended. At first, it seemed nothing more than a pit waited below the last step, but it was simply a slab of onyx so dark as to allow no reflection, not even of Cassilda's magical light.

A short passageway led them up to a final door, though this one was not magical. Heavy, carved from some nameless wood, with a ring-handle fashioned from black metal. Cassilda pulled open the door with a hand that trembled ever so slightly.

The door swung open, and they stepped into the vaults

The vaults were not one room, but a series of chambers connected by small corridors, resembling the multiple stomachs of a camelid. If the contents of each room were organised by some governing principle or theme, Cassilda could not discern what that was. Great piles of glittering gold, silver, bronze, and gemstones lay next to pieces of rusted metal twisted in unfathomable shapes. Delicate tiaras sat atop gnarled machines that looked like the skeletons of antediluvian beasts.

Real skeletons also dwelt in this place, huge bones so large they could be mistaken for pillars supporting the low, oppressive ceiling. Cassilda recognised the scorpion-like carapaces of eurypterids, polished to a marble gleam and arrayed like segments of burnished armour, and shuddered recalling their sojourn through the labyrinth of Namtar's Temple and confrontation with one of the ancient horrors there. There were also plates from a gigantic arthropleura, the bones of dimetrodons, and other creatures she did not recognise.

"Wait, wait!" Petruccio said.

They came to a halt.

"What is it?" Cassilda said.

"We must slow down. We're already five rooms deep."

Cassilda frowned. That did not seem right. In her own mind, they had only just begun to explore the second room.

"But this is . . . " LeBarron trailed off. He looked behind him, as did Cassilda, and they saw the dwarf was right. Five open doorways, each framed within the last like an endless series of reflected mirrors, trailed back to the solid wooden door that marked the entrance. Cassilda blinked. Was this the product of her mind wandering or something more sinister? She had explored these vaults as a child, had she not? She did not remember time slipping away so. *But then, time moves differently for children. They occupy an eternal now. Hours vanish if their attention is on something.* And Cassilda, knowing from birth her lifespan would be eternal bar injury, had not feared the passage of time.

"I do not like this," LeBarron said. "The vaults should not stretch in one direction like this. Surely, a loop would be more efficient, or a clockface, with multiple chambers leading off from a central point... That the vaults are organised in a single file seems, well, peculiar."

"Ominous, more like," Petruccio said. "It forces us to keep going, and the farther in we go, the longer it will take to get back."

"Time is of the essence," Cassilda said. "So we must not go too deep. We should set a limit on how many rooms we explore. No more than twenty."

They continued, a slow and poisonous dread spreading from their hearts to their extremities. The vaults were freezing, and it seemed as they went on they grew darker—though Cassilda could observe no logical reason for this—the shadows wrapping these abandoned talismans in thicker, more furtive shadows. Strange amulets winked from corners where darkness gathered like pools of oil. Rings glittered on the fingers of mummified beings that sat on dark thrones, sightlessly watching the party as they made their way deeper. Automatons, crude contraptions of steel and wire and bags full of sickly ichor, lurched out of the shadows, their mannequin faces appealing to Cassilda, as though they wished to be taken from this darkness up to the light.

"Pause here," Petruccio said. Sweat sheened his brow. Cassilda realised it was the mental exertion of maintaining his sense of time. "We have reached twenty rooms."

"But we barely spent thirty seconds here!" LeBarron hissed. "Why then are my legs so tired. Oh by the Black Star!"

"Hush, LeBarron, lest you wake sleepers here," Cassilda said, beginning to fear the inanimate things that dwelt here, for nothing was truly inanimate, everything a vessel for imminence, and she feared that divine imminence might strike at any moment, giving these cloth-bound corpses and metal-clad puppets life. "We must go a little farther. We have found nothing of any use."

"I cannot," LeBarron said. "I cannot."

Petruccio clapped a hand on LeBarron's shoulder.

"You can and you will, LeBarron. Are you not the bearer of *Hope Reborn*? Are you not a hero of Carcosa?"

The mummer looked at the sword, which hung at his side like a cruel pet, eager to be played with. The sword seemed very at home down here, in the chasmal darkness, with the other grim artefacts still bearing the traces of their makers' obsession. The sword might have been renamed *Hope Reborn*, but there was no forgetting its original name: *Hope's Devourer*.

"I will go on," LeBarron said, at last. "But before I do, there is something I have to tell you. I don't know why it must be now, but something about this place compels me."

"Can it not wait? Cali marches upon us!" Cassilda hissed.

"It must be now," LeBarron said. His eyes darted about, as if seeing things in the shadows the others could not. "I can no longer bear it. And it may be useful in what's to come."

"If it is useful, you would have done well to have told us before," Petruccio growled.

"It is no good crying once the wine is already spilled," LeBarron snapped, though even his retorts were hushed—all of them keeping their voices low, for fear of disturbing *something,* none of them knew what.

"Proceed, LeBarron," Cassilda said, trying to inject her voice with kindness, all the while her skin crawling with fear and anticipation.

LeBarron drew a deep breath.

"When I died, in Alar . . . I crossed over to the other side."

"You said you could not speak of what you saw there," Cassilda reminded him.

LeBarron nodded.

"But we come to the end of the world, dear princess. All vows must be forsaken for the final and ultimate vow to be fulfilled, for the last truth to be spoken, for the True Self to be realised."

His voice had the fervency of a preacher, the madness of a prophet, and Cassilda realised that's exactly what he was. LeBarron had many times predicted—albeit obliquely—various destinies within their tightly woven party. He had known from the beginning that Alan Chambers was more than a man. He had called Cali the Queen in Black long before she became so. Cassilda wondered whether this gift of prophecy was tied to his role as a mummer, for the mummer was a receptacle of truth, not a solid object but a vessel designed to be filled up with inspiration—not unlike the inanimate objects that she had been thinking about moments before. The actor made themselves invisible so that another face might be seen. The actor destroyed their own voice so that another might speak through them. Perhaps LeBarron had so perfectly hollowed himself that the waters of the universe could not help but flow into him, as they might into a beautifully sculpted urn, revealing the secrets forbidden to most minds.

"Beyond death, *he* was. Alan Chambers! Yes. I saw him there, Cassilda. Perhaps it was a premonition of his fate. But I don't think so. There, time stopped moving forward. It was more like the waters of time were converging in the heart of a whirlpool, sucked down into a point where . . . where everything was One! And Alan, he was part of that Oneness. No . . . He *was* that Oneness."

"Stop," Cassilda said. Though she kept her voice low, the howl of pain could still be heard. "Stop. I cannot bear it anymore. You speak as if he shall come back from the dead, but none save my father return from beyond the Two Towers of Death." Tears ran down her face. "And even He, now, has failed to return. So do not speak to me of resurrections. The only hope rests with us."

"No, Cassilda," LeBarron said. He gripped her arm, a fevered madness making his eyes almost as bright as her magical light. "No, you're wrong. He is beyond Death! I know it. I've been keeping the truth down this whole time, but in the void, all things come into being, and what is this place other than a void? Everything that has been lost will one day be found again."

"Speak to me no more." She turned her face away and wrenched her arm from his grip. "I shall hear no more fantasies."

He was not a prophet, after all, merely grief-struck like she was, driven out of sanity by the dogs of despair. No, she could not listen to him.

LeBarron hung his head. The light seemed to go out of his eyes. He stood as still as any of the mannequins in the dark, as though a gorgon had turned him to stone.

"We should only venture a little farther," Petruccio said, with forced evenness. "Five or so rooms. No more."

Cassilda nodded. They set off, LeBarron eventually followed, moving every bit like the lifeless golem he had come to resemble.

It was in the twenty-second room they found something of use.

The thing glittered even before Cassilda's light fell upon it. At first, she thought it might have been a ghost, a bright, spectral form hiding in the corner of the room, but its brightness, though shimmering, had a hard quality to it that excluded the possibility of mere spirit. Was it teeth? Pearls? No, pearl shone and gleamed, but did not glitter quite like this. Ice perhaps?

The proper shape of the thing steadily came into view the nearer they approached. No wonder Cassilda had mistaken it for a ghost, for it had legs, arms, a torso, even a head—but no, these weren't limbs and body-parts, rather they were pieces of armour made to be fitted to them. A full suit of priceless plating, complete with pauldrons, tassets, vambraces, cuirass, gorget, and helm. And finally, as her light washed over the sparkling suit, igniting the surface the way the sun could illuminate a cavern of crystal, she finally discerned what it was made of: neither eurypterid chitin nor dragon-scale, neither magical metal nor hide of mythical beast. It was something far simpler, yet more awe-inspiring because of that.

Diamond.

But the strangest thing of all about the armour was that it was made for one of Petruccio's stature. The dwarf stared at the magnificent platemail in awe and wonder.

"I've always known there were others like me," he said. "But it is rare to find something like this fashioned for the sake of a dwarf." Petruccio stroked the platemail's surface with his callous fingers; a studded texture, resembling the hide of a lizard rendered in pure radiance. "I wonder who its original bearer was?" He looked around him, no longer with the fear they all shared, but a little of wonder. "Or whether there *was* an original bearer at all, and this place provided it for me . . . "

Cassilda smiled sadly, for his words evoked the memory of a child she had long since lost.

"Perhaps that is the truth of it. Nothing about this place is familiar to me from when I used to walk its halls as a child. Maybe the vaults are more like a mind, Carcosa's mind, and these are the dreams it has discarded, serving up to us now in our hour of need."

Petruccio smiled.

"Why not? If I was not mad when I first came to Carcosa, eighty years here have surely driven me to it. Why insist upon reality where no such reality exists?" A single tear formed at the corner of the dwarf's eye, but he would not let it fall. "Alan might have said something like that."

"He might," Cassilda conceded. "I don't know what the future holds, but I know that this armour was made for you. It would be an affront to that which men call God not to take it."

Petruccio nodded.

"Will you help me put it on?"

"Yes."

"Then we must go." LeBarron's voice almost shocked Cassilda, it was so strong, so confident, so bold. When she looked at him, his fever and fear seemed to have dissipated, replaced by a hardness like the very diamond that twinkled before them.

He truly is a chameleon, taking on whatever substance or texture surrounds him, she thought. *That is why he loved Alan so, for Alan inspired him to a better self.*

"We need a weapon that can defeat Cali," Petruccio said. "This armour is useful, but it is not what we came here for."

"We already have a weapon that can defeat Cali," LeBarron said. He touched the handle of the sword at his belt. "We have had it all this time. You say that I will not get within reach of her, but I say that is cowardice. This place will show us a thousand rooms, and we will never find a weapon to defeat her, because we already possess all that we need."

"LeBarron, my words to you earlier were harsh. It is not wrong to dream of the return of those we love. I just . . . did not want to get lost in illusion."

LeBarron bowed.

"Your apology is gratefully accepted, dear princess. But you were right: we cannot rely on false hope. Alan isn't coming back. I am a poor substitute, but we must make do with what we have. I shall try to play his role, to face Cali and slay her, as he was always meant to do. And if it be my final performance, then so be it!"

"No, LeBarron." Cassilda and the mummer turned in surprise at Petruccio's words; the dwarf's eyes had not left the glittering suit of diamond, its glory reflected in his ever-dark pupils, like a secret world in the dark mirror of a magician. "It is not only your responsibility, but all of ours. We are *Il Triello*. Our three must become one. If yours is the blade that shall strike at her, then mine is the shield that shall defend us." At last, his eyes left the magical armour, and fixed upon the princess. "And you, Cassilda, you shall be the living heart of vengeance."

Cassilda smiled.

She could not disagree.

CHAPTER 10
ZOS THE DREAMER

T
HE GARDEN AT night was like a dream, forever unfolding, revealing new and stranger dimensions. Abracadabra's sense of continuity was continually being undermined as he found himself thrust into the middle of stories without beginning or end. Had he not, but moments before, danced with moths bearing the faces of children? O how he had laughed to see them! But now here he was, drinking from a pool while great multicoloured toads croaked reproachfully beside him, their baleful eyes turned upward in worship of the stars. How had he gotten here from there? And what would the next moment reveal? Stones that sang ageless songs. Grass that laughed as it bent in the wind . . .

He wandered. Some shapes he recognised among the flora: harsh moon-clowns and succulent disberries. Others grew into archetypes he did not have a name for. He prayed before them in awe, sometimes naming them with the reverence of Adam, who, alone of all mankind—even Christ—remained unborn.

"Why, hello."

Abracadabra turned. The pool and the toads were gone. He stood in what seemed less a garden and more a meadow, a bright yellow field full of crop that might have been wheat, though it grew only to his waist. Opposite him stood a man with strange features, both wild and exceedingly cultivated in equal measure. A strong jawline and thin lips gave his face a sternness that contrasted with his frazzled, wild hair—hair that travelled upward without assistance as though it was being stimulated by electrical current. The man wore a country blazer and suit trousers, the kind an aristocrat living on a manor estate might sport, yet his eyes burned, as though fire had been trapped in the form of opalescent gems and inserted into his sockets.

Trees hemmed Abracadabra and the newcomer—though he supposed *he* was the real newcomer—in this field. At first, he thought that the perimeter of trees formed a square, but in truth he was inside a triangle. For some reason, this perturbed and excited him.

"You must be Abracadabra," the man said. "My name while living was Austin, though, as I'm sure you're aware, such names mean very little here. I'd prefer you call me Zos."

"Zos," Abracadabra said, testing the word. It held an ungraspable, mysterious quality. "Is the name of your own devising?"

Zos smiled.

"To answer that question, you shall first have to say what you mean by 'your own'. What, precisely, do we own? Mind? Ego? Spirit? Or perhaps nothing at all." Zos walked slowly towards Abracadabra, running his fingers through the gloriously bright yellow crops as he did so, smiling a smile so soft that it could not but melt Abracadabra's fears away, the rigidity leaving his body with the ease of water sluicing from a jug.

"We own nothing, because there is no 'I'," Abracadabra said.

"But do you truly comprehend that truth?" Zos was only a few steps from him now, and Abracadabra had a sudden premonition—a thrill of secret pleasure mixed with a kind of terror—that Zos might reach out and touch him. Zos's smile was undeniably sensuous. The hard lines of his face, that moments before seemed such a contrast with the wilderness of his hair and eyes, now seemed a different kind of firmness, the surety of a lover, a master of the physical world.

"I suppose I haven't internalised it yet," Abracadabra said. "I still feel I have . . . an identity."

"And that is okay," Zos reassured, now easily within touching distance, but—for whatever reason—Zos did not reach out just yet. "All of us have a sense of Self, and that never leaves, even when one pierces the illusion, even when one dissolves all polarities, going beyond pleasure . . . " He let out a sigh that very much suggested there was pleasure in going beyond pleasure. "But for you the veil still occludes the truth, still hides you from the face of the One."

"The One?" Abracadabra trembled.

"Yes, the One. The first, the eternal, the preeminent, the all-encompassing. To perceive the One, you must dissolve your barriers, you must open yourself to *all* things, even things hateful to you, even things you are afraid of. Some call this atavism; I call it love!"

Zos spread his arms, and from him there shone a deep red light, though alternating sometimes to a warm amber. His flesh kindled with flame, great tongues of fire licking from him. He was a martyr aflame in the heart of a golden sea, an effigy burning in the darkest night. A roar sounded somewhere in the foundations of the earth. The garden's nocturnal dwellers called out as one, a baying of orgasmic jubilation. Then, the light faded, and Abracadabra's eyes stung for lack of its beauty.

"You are a dream," Abracadabra said, the words spilling from his lips involuntarily. "A dream made flesh!"

Zos smiled.

"Yes. I am your dream, in one sense. I represent the dreaming state. In dream, there are no ethical boundaries, no obstacles of logic. Men may mate with monsters, and women may take beasts to their bed. Their offspring, the therianthropes, are the children of dream. You are one such dream-child. Though you look like a man, truly you walk with the zigzag of the serpent. Though you speak like a man, yours is the serpent's hiss."

"But I still feel shame," Abracadabra confessed. "I remember my deeds, and I think of what I am, how strange it is, and there is something that repulses me."

"Repulsion is just another part of the cosmic dance of pleasure. Cali knows that all too well. It is one of her many strengths."

"How can I defeat her?"

"Defeat?" Zos seemed confused, then a smile illuminated his quixotic features. "Ah yes, I suppose you must. I should have done it myself, but she once gave me such pleasure: not purely of the flesh, but of the spirit too."

"You seem . . . very fixated on pleasure." The opposite of Andrew whom he'd met a moment before—and also a lifetime ago.

Austin—or rather Zos—smiled again.

"I wrote the book on pleasure." His eyes twinkled with a form of mischief. "But come, these are the statements of ego, and ego must be discarded before the final revelation. For ego separates.

Like the sword, it divides us from truth. You are almost there, Abracadabra. You have but to realise there is no separateness."

"But *how*?"

Zos took a final step toward him, now standing so close Abracadabra could feel his soft breath upon his cheek, could smell his scent, which was a mixture of a thousand different flowers, each more subtle and enticing than the last.

"Easily."

Zos planted his lips upon Abracadabra's, and for a moment, a surge of panic filled Abracadabra's mind. *No! This is a man. This can't be right. This isn't you!*

His thoughts quieted, and he instead concentrated on the profound softness of the lips locked to his, of the delicacy with which Zos's tongue explored, of the taste—sandalwood and smoke and strawberries—that sent a flush of pleasure down his throat and into his groin. *I can't be . . . I can't be aroused . . . I'm straight . . .* But such thoughts held no weight against the experience itself. They were as effectual as the vain barking of a dog in a far away valley. He had defined himself with all these hollow terms: man, straight, married, failure, white, but none of them held any meaning, and at last he understood what Zos had been trying to teach him.

The taste Abracadabra found to be so sweet upon Zos's lips was his own. The joy he felt was the joy of self-discovery, of meeting his own soul upon a dark road, and knowing himself for who he was. His shame was shed from him, like a heavy winter cloak discarded at the approach of the summer sun. He stood in the full, beaming light of his own consciousness and realised the profound power of his own freedom. He kissed Zos back, as passionately as he had ever kissed anyone, and felt a flame kindle in his own soul with the ferocity of ignited oil. Crown to toe he pulsed with the newfound light of his own self-creation.

Their lips parted, and Abracadabra opened his eyes.

He stood alone in the golden field.

The pain he felt was like waking from a dream.

CHAPTER 11
SATURNINE

NIGHT FELL AS Cali reached the gates of Carcosa, the twilight casting the twisted spires of the hideous citadel in a lunatic's pallor. Cali almost shed a tear, the awesome nature of the moment nearly dragging her into a deep undertow of emotion. She had dreamed so often of this day, of returning to the city with an army at her back, of finally claiming Carcosa for her own. She stood before the city of her father not as supplicant but as master. She did not come to beg its forgiveness, but to demand its submission. Her will was absolute, and her power as eternal as the Black Star. Indeed, dreadful Aldebaran beamed down upon her, like a benediction from beyond the void.

The gate's destruction had been hastily offset with crude scaffolding. She saw speartips glinting in the starlight. The city was not asleep; they waited for her in readiness. She expected nothing less. Her sister no doubt had found her way back to Carcosa and warned them of Cali's coming.

Cali gritted her teeth. This time, she would not let Cassilda escape. A reflux of sisterly affection had caused her to hesitate back in the Six-Ringed City—Cali always had struggled with her emotions. But not this time. She was clearheaded for the first time in millennia. Bizarrely, it was the deaths of the children that had freed her thoughts from their lingering burdens. The right brain, with its propensity for imagination and fantasy and sentiment, had forever misguided her. But now she governed herself according to the lefthand way, the way of logic and progress and science. She had learned this truth in part from Pe'kar—and that itself was a wisdom: one could learn from their enemies. Her sister had taught her much, as had Pe'kar, and the fool Alan Chambers. Did not kings keep jesters precisely for this reason? Idiots often stumbled upon profundity, if only by accident. When her rule was established, she would be sure to keep a few fools at court, maybe LeBarron could serve such a purpose, as well as fulfilling other needs . . .

He may be too dangerous to allow to live. If that was the case, she would kill him. Her heart wouldn't bleed. She no longer felt emotion for those she killed. If more children had to die, then so be it. If Carcosa's population had to be decimated, then so be it. If she had to level every brick of the city to ensure she ruled supreme, then so be it. Hers was the right to unite the black planet. Her goal was in reach, and she knew what steps must be taken to ensure it was achieved.

"Your orders, my queen?" Malebolge snarled. He was, in many respects, a parody of demonkind, the kind of bestial archetype depicted in the primitive manuscripts of medieval priests and monks. Cali supposed all stereotypes had their source, one way or another.

"Keep the army in readiness of the attack," she said. "When the wall comes down, commit all forces to the assault."

Malebolge's eyes widened.

"When . . . when the wall comes down, my queen?"

Cali smiled.

"You have heard the words of your empress."

The demon bowed, then took to the skies, circling with others of his kind, spreading the message among the trueborn to be relayed to the further reaches of the army. One last time, she permitted herself to survey her legions. A glorious host, perhaps the largest that had ever been raised on the black planet. Tens of thousands of infantry readied themselves, marshalling like a colony of ants detecting the presence of a rival nest. Their armour and weaponry glinted like starfire stolen from the black of night. Their eyes conveyed the hunger of rabid dogs. Al Shujah had not been enough for them. The tiny town was overwhelmed with barely a tenth of her force. Many had failed to find action, and that had only increased their bloodlust.

Then there were the horrors of Pe'kar's experiments. These, she knew, were unpredictable. One or two of them had already caused minor havoc in the ranks. One exploded after gorging themselves on too many corpses in Al Shujah, incinerating several hundred of her men. Another was found laying eggs in the ear canals of her warriors. What hatched from the eggs was no lifeform Cali recognised—she quickly stamped them out in fear they might become uncontrollable.

But once these freaks were unleashed upon Carcosa, their unreliability would matter little. They would sow chaos and disorder, exhausting the already spent energies of the Carcosan army.

She had set aside another regiment of elite warriors to guard the ark containing The Claw. They were the only squadron in her army she intended to hold back. For if The Claw fell into the wrong hands, it could prove disastrous.

The only way she knew of destroying The Claw was in the very fires it was made: the Fires of Manifestation. However, there was great danger in bringing it into the city before she was certain her path was clear. Thus, the Warriors of the Ark would hold back, allowing her legions to carve a path to the palace, where she might finally obliterate The Claw—and all threat to her—for good.

"Forward," Cali said, at last. Satan obliged, padding slowly towards the dilapidated gateway of the city she had once called home. Carcosa's architecture loomed ruinously over her, somehow more intimidating at night, as though the city were a shapeshifter, wearing a new bestiality with the rising of the moon. However much she outnumbered the Carcosans, however powerful she had become, she knew this fight would not be easy. Though her pride still awoke upon occasion, she had subdued its passions and fantasies. The battle before her would be the toughest and greatest she had ever fought. Cassilda would not relinquish the city to her easily, and for all her flaws, her sister was resilient. *Stubborn, more like*. Almost to stupidity. But Cali could not deny Cassilda had courage. It was one of the few things they shared.

And Petruccio, he will be here as well. She'd always thought she had the measure of the dwarf, yet so often he surprised her. She had taught him superficial magics, but she suspected he had been able to take his study deeper when not under her watchful eye. *There is no way he can match your power. Not even in a hundred years of study*.

She now stood perhaps three hundred feet from the gate. She saw, with perfect night-vision, the soldiers watching her from the wall. She could hear their breaths held, their pulses quickening. Their eyes never left her.

"Warriors of Carcosa!" she cried, projecting her voice with magic so that it reverberated louder than the church bells of Carcosa during times of war. Though those bells now remained eerily silent. What did that indicate? Some ploy of Cassilda's? Or simply the hanging silence before the storm . . .

"Warriors," she continued. "My quarrel is not with you. It is with my sister, who as long as I have lived colluded with my father to deny me even the simplest things due a child from their parent: love, respect, safety." Her voice trembled for a moment, the mortal in her surfacing; then the god returned, subsuming her fear and fragility. "Many of you, I trained with. Some I schooled in the arts of war. Unlike my sister, I have walked *all* of Carcosa's streets, from the markets of the coprophages to the high spires of the courtiers, from the orreries of the wise stargazers to the shanties of the cannibals. I have participated in the great drama of the city. I have been one of you!" She paused a moment, letting this final word ring with the clarion of a trumpet. "Now, I return to the city of my birth, not as a princess, nor as a general, but as a god. I slew Pe'kar, the Demon King, and took his power from him. The war between Carcosa and the land of Blue Light is ended. Open your gates, and your hearts, and I shall shower you with the gifts only a deity can bestow!" Her eyes darkened, like eclipsed suns, a fell half-light that spoke of deep magic. "But if you deny me, if you bar me entry, if you—like my sister—deny me the kingdom that is not only my birthright, but a right I have earned with service and devotion, then I shall show you the fury of the Demon Queen! I shall break this proud city, rubble its spires, tear up its foundations, and reign blood from the heavens. There is no need for more death. Carcosa has known enough of war. Open your gates and turn over my sister to me—and you shall know the generosity of Cali!"

She finished, nearly breathless, not from the effort of projection but from controlling the tide of emotions that surged beneath the words.

For a long moment, there was no answer. Carcosa stood silent as a gravestone, or perhaps an artist lost in the deranged splendour of their own creation, and then an answer came, a sound Cali had dreaded, loathed, that awoke in her all the feelings she had thought banished by her ascension to the throne of the Demon King.

Laughter.

"Let me, Abratax, answer you on behalf of the city, Cali." The warrior spat her name as though it were less than a curse, less than dogshit upon his heel. "Carcosa knows no lord except the King In Yellow—*Deathless is He!* We bow to none but Almighty Hastur, whose wisdom has guided us through the ages. And even should He not return, His memory shall make a better ruler than you! These gates will not open to you. This city shall fight you to its last breath. But methinks it is not the city that shall breathe its last, but *you,* false god! It is not our pride that shall be broken, but yours! All hail the King In Yellow!"

A thousand voices answered him, their thunder causing the hair to rise on Cali's arms. She hated herself in that moment, hated her own flesh for how it betrayed her, for the organism, it seemed, still held the memory of fear. How dare this ingrate, this mere servant, mock her before the gates of her city? She trembled. She had known many rages, some blacker than night, some more volcanic than the planet's core. But this rage was different, for it was a moonbright rage, a rage of madness and dream-fever, as though she had consumed the noxious flesh of mushrooms, inhaled the acrid smoke of powdered drugs. Her mind—so carefully directed along the railroad of logic—derailed itself with the kamikaze momentum of a charging bull. Conscious thought winked away like an extinguished candle, leaving only a roiling blackness without beginning or end.

"Then die!" she screamed.

What Cali did next was heard across the black planet. Tales would be sung of it, poems composed, and performances given by mummers ardent for glory. Some magicians claimed that the sound could still be heard centuries afterwards, never dying out, a death-scream trapped in time by magic and memory.

Cali raised her harp high over her head, and with a single brush of her hand struck a chord that resonated with chthonian power. For a moment it seemed the OM of the universe faltered in its guttural peal, galaxies gliding to a halt as the void trembled, remembering what it had once been before life was spurted into its womb. Deeper than hell was the note, deeper than the foundations of all matter and being. Had Cali been able to sustain such a sound, perhaps reality itself would have come undone, perhaps the veil of the material would have pulled back to reveal the glittering, gemlike depths of true existence. But as it was, the note sounded for merely a few seconds, no more than a breath.

Such brevity was enough to make the black planet quake, the great city groan, and then with a noise like the roar of a wounded dragon the walls of Carcosa ruptured, then broke entirely, crashing to the ground with tectonic impact. Rubble hailed. Screams were swallowed by the gurgle of churning rock. Stones that had stood for eons crumbled into ashen dust. The earth received the mountainous payload and quaked once more, as if for fear.

For a moment, even Cali recoiled at what she had done. She had destroyed more than mere stone; she had destroyed a piece of her father's dream, wrought by the brush of Uboth. *Some things were never meant to be undone!* Pull at the wrong thread, and the entire cloth will disintegrate. *What have you done?*

But a dark voice answered her. *You have done what you must. Now, claim the city. End this once and for all!*

Perhaps a thousand Carcosans had perished with the destruction of the walls alone. Those not dead were either buried beneath stone or howling in agony, limbs and bones crushed to powder. Now was the moment to attack, to swoop upon the city like a swift plague, for it lay defenceless as a newborn, cold flesh exposed to the wild elements.

But she saw a figure standing above the rubble. Saturnine, he loomed with the awe-inspiring presence of a demigod. Briefly, she wondered if Pe'kar had not returned, having performed some astounding ruse. But no, this figure was more haggard than the perfect Demon King, a grizzled, scar-torn effigy of bloodshed and ruin, whose lank hair framed a face skeletal as death's incarnate image. All at once, she knew who he was, who dared to oppose her even now, and a smile came to her lips.

"I had almost forgotten that there are two kings in Carcosa," Cali said.

The figure—flesh pale as the moon's ghost—answered her naught, save to step down from the rubble of the walls, and stand before the broken defences in the posture of Cerberus, guarding the secrets of hell. The challenger was around seven foot tall, but he seemed ten times that, a hulking giant, a titan escaped from Tartarus.

Cali laughed as he came toward her. Now *this* would be a battle worthy of record. She hoped LeBarron watched from some hidden vantage, for she would demand he compose a verse describing this moment. No one, thus far, had been able to rival her power for even a minute. She hoped—prayed even—that this gaunt warrior might prove different.

She kicked Satan's flanks, and the gorgonopsid padded forward. She put aside her harp and drew her long, cruel blade.

Her foe came on, dauntless of either steed or rider.

Cali smiled again. One more name to her legend.

The Cannibal King had risen to defend his city.

CHAPTER 12
WOE

C ASSILDA HEARD THE city scream, and she screamed with it. Upon the slopes of the palace steppe, she, LeBarron, and Petruccio froze like silverfish paralysed by the thud of a stick upon the ground. The note that no hand or throat should ever have made had sounded, so pestilential it seemed a festering boil upon the psychosphere, upon memory itself; with it came a cacophonous, gurgling wail as the walls crumbled, buckling as though their last strength had perished. Stone once thought solid deluged like tidal waters upon the city's buildings and streets. Sky-clawing spires trembled. Towers shook and cracked. The mycelial domes and mosques writhed and flinched as titanic force ruptured the very earth upon which they were founded. Dust rose like a sandstorm and choked the streets and sky, blotting the stars. Avalanches of rubble buried fleeing souls. Screams sounded from every corner of the gargantuan city. Then came the wail of the prophets and mummers.

"*Doom! Doom! Doom! The Black Empress is come!*"

Cassilda fell to her knees, drained of all hope. She wept. The only glimmer of gladness she could find was that Alan Chambers had died before he could witness the end of this great city.

But then she felt a hand upon her shoulder. Her eyes met Petruccio's, which in the midst of the black dust clouds rising from the decimated streets below shone like a fallen star. He and his armour seemed one, a creature of diamond skin, blazing out amidst the destruction, a sparkling iridescence produced by the collapse of the city, a supernova from a dying star.

"If this is the end, dear princess, then I would have us end straight-backed and proud. We may not be able to stop Cali, not if she can level the very walls . . . " He swallowed down the bolus of emotion that threatened to crack his facade. "But we can meet her in battle. We can show her we are not afraid. I could die happy, knowing I had done that."

The smallest smile quirked his lips.

Cassilda returned the smile, though tears still streamed down her face.

"Tell me, Petruccio. How is it that you came to be stronger than the very stone of Carcosa? You are a wonder of the world."

Petruccio's smile remained, though his eyes changed, becoming watery pools filled with distorted reflections; scenes, perhaps, from a past he did not wish revealed.

"Diamonds are formed by constant pressure, my princess." Then his jaw became a blade's edge, so firmly was it set. "No, my *Queen*." He extended a hand. Cassilda felt her heart thunder in her chest. She had been in denial for so long, but she could not deny it any longer, not with the walls coming down, not with her sister at the gate. Her father was not coming back, nor was Alan. She was the Queen of Carcosa. On her, everything rested.

Taking Petruccio's hand, she rose.

"To the very last," she said.

Petruccio bowed.

"To the very last."

"Woe," LeBarron whispered, like one rehearsing lines from a play, and indeed he was, for Cassilda recognised the words of *The King In Yellow,* spoken perhaps for the last time in the city of their making. "You have seized the throne and the empire. Woe to you who are crowned!"

CHAPTER 13
THE ALL-CONQUERING CHILD

ABRACADABRA HAD MET two ghosts of Cali's past, now it was time to meet the third. A dreadful anxiety came over him, fearing that this last visitor would be—like in the Dickens tale—the most strange and frightening of all.

As the darkness deepened, and the nightside of Eden unveiled its full gothic resplendence, Abracadabra searched for his last visitor with mounting desperation. His nerves jangled like the bells of some demented church. It wasn't only fear, but a sense of time slipping away, as though this night would see no dawn, would only deepen and deepen to a point of absolute blackness, a return to the un-creation of the beginning. He had to find the visitor before then!

There! In the treeline beyond. A white ghost. That must be the third visitor, but why was he looking away? Abracadabra took a step toward the figure. The ghost fled before him. Abracadabra followed as fast as his feet could carry him. He ran like a panther through the dark forest, leaping over roots and fallen trunks, slipping between narrow corridors formed by thorny briars. Breathless, sweat-sleek, he bounded through the garden, eyes never leaving the flitting spirit. *Where is he leading me?* he wondered. Perhaps simply on a merry chase. Perhaps nowhere. Perhaps to the end of time itself.

Just as with his goals in life—that former life before the garden—the harder he chased the spirit, the farther the spirit seemed to get away; it was a paradox that surely The King would have delighted in: in reaching to grasp an object one only proved beyond question its unreality. *By saying "I want this thing" I reinforce the fact I do not have it. Desire is my barrier. Desire is my Achilles Heel!*

Abracadabra stopped—so suddenly that the momentum almost carried him face-first into the dirt. Swaying slightly, he took deep breaths, regaining balance and equilibrium.

And then he heard a voice behind him.

"Very good. Love must always come under will, after all."

Slowly, Abracadabra turned.

He came face to face with one of the strangest looking men he had ever seen; strange, because he seemed not one but two people, visible through one another like two illustrations drawn on tracing paper and then overlaid; each version of the man permeated the other, the way yin and yang were interpenetrated, their essences conjoined yet distinct. The first of these two characters—although who could really say which was first or last—was tall, imposing, regal in the way of a military commander. He was dressed smartly like a twentieth century gentleman in blazer, waistcoat, and bowtie. Hook-nosed and austere, he resembled a hawk, his domed, shaven scalp only adding to the impression of a bird of prey overseeing a vast domain from the peak of a mountain. His eyes were so penetrating, Abracadabra could scarcely tolerate their attention.

The second figure was altogether different. Unkempt, long-haired, like a scraggy dog brought in from the rain. Indeed, this figure seemed hunched, cretinous, as though he had been raised by wolves and never quite civilised by human society. All he wore were soiled rags, though they were colourful beneath the dirt, like Joseph's cloak of many hues, signifying an inner magical being. Where the first figure had a portly physique, augmenting his already imposing presence, this second man was rake-thin, a malnourished scavenger haunting the ruins of a necropolis. Both moved as one, though neither had recourse to blink.

"Who are you?" Abracadabra asked.

"I am Aleister."

"I am Therion."

The two answered simultaneously. The hawk-nosed man sniffed. He appeared to be Aleister. The other doglike wretch was Therion.

"Why are there two of you?"

Aleister smiled. Therion spat.

"Have you come so far and learned nothing of *polarity,* my dear boy?" Aleister intoned. It seemed Therion was content to let his counterpart answer this question. He produced a small bone—

the source of which Abracadabra could not identify—and began to gnaw on it, his rotten teeth making a *clunk clunk clunk* noise on the marrow.

"Polarity?"

"Balance is needed in all things. Yin and yang, Horus and Set . . . "

"Horus, the Egyptian god?"

"Yes. He and his uncle, Set—though often they are thought of as twins—are not enemies, as told in the myth. In reality, they are one god, the god of double-power, the ceaseless opposition of the universe that gives birth to our very senses, our entire framework of perception. For, how could perception exist without contrast? That is the first created thing, my dear boy: God separated the waters." Aleister's eyes bored into Abracadabra's. Still, he had not blinked.

"So, we all have these two sides within us, is that what you're saying?"

Aleister huffed. Therion threw away his bone and snapped.

"*Idiot! Moron! Have you not been listening! There is no two!*"

Abracadabra blinked. His eyes were hurting from taking in Aleister-Therion's double-form, though according to them it was not double, but a unified whole where opposites met. Or maybe that was only an aspiration, not something fully attained. Perhaps that was the lesson.

"*He doesn't get it,*" Therion snarled, addressing his words to Aleister. "*He thinks in dualities. He's useless!*"

"Come, my dear Therion, he cannot be entirely useless. How else could he have made it here?"

Therion growled, but made no answer. He retrieved another bone from his pocket and began to gnaw again.

"Will you walk with me?" Aleister said, politely.

Abracadabra nodded. The two—or rather three—fell into step. Therion trailed behind, regularly stopping to sniff a tree, or pick up what looked to Abracadabra like useless pieces of wood, once even pulling up the front of his robe and pissing on a bush. If Aleister was perturbed by his double's activities, he showed no sign.

"I feel like the longer I spend in the garden, the *less* I understand the truth," Abracadabra said. "When I first came here, I felt like I was on the cusp of something—I guess you could call it enlightenment. It feels silly, now."

"There's nothing silly about it. Samdhi. Enlightenment. Attainment. These are all words for aspiration to something greater, to the realisation of one's total being." Aleister's eyes stared straight ahead, seeming to pierce all veils. "Every man or woman is a star, Abracadabra. We have it in us to take our place in the night sky." Suddenly he swivelled, and Abracadabra nearly fell over, feeling as though he were in the talons of a brilliant, wrathful eagle. Aleister was so close, Abracadabra could smell his breath— a metallic scent. "But it seems *you* are rather experiencing a dark night of the soul."

Abracadabra looked around him at the garden, shrouded in the deepest night he had ever known. A small smile crept to his lips.

"*He begins to understand,*" Therion barked.

"I think he does," Aleister said.

"But if what I am afraid of *is* true, how can I . . . "

"Go on living sanely?"

Abracadabra nodded.

Aleister laughed, a harsh, staccato sound that pierced the cloying penumbra of night.

"You can't. But that is alright, for the world is not sane. God is not sane. The true condition of all things is a form of total, blissful insanity. Sanity is what resists this rhythm of life, like a stubborn stone fallen into a river, damming up its flow. You must cast sanity—and a great deal of other things—aside if you want to return, and if you want to face *her*."

His voice dripped with contempt that seemed quite out of place. Abracadabra had heard Andrew's righteous fury, Austin's sadness and passion, but Aleister's rage seemed incongruous with the magic and serenity of the garden, like a wrong note in the night-song of the birds.

"I don't know how to defeat Cali," Abracadabra said.

Therion spat and cursed.

"*Throw him away, Aleister. He is useless!*"

Aleister smiled, but there was a terrible sorrow in his eyes, as though all the pain of the world had been condensed into these two frozen gemstones.

"If I knew how, my dear boy, I would have done it myself. Alas, she was too much for me."

"*Coward! Weakling! You are no master!*" Therion snarled. Aleister accepted this abuse with surprising submissiveness.

"Can I ask you something?"

"Of course," Aleister said.

"Were you the first?" Abracadabra asked.

Aleister let out a monosyllabic bark of laughter. For a moment, he'd sounded eerily like his other self.

"Of course, not. Before me there was Ambrose, and before him another, an endless line stretching back to the crack of doom." Aleister pondered a moment. "But I was . . . special to her, I suppose. She was my angel, my whore. And I was her servant. For a time, at least." His glimmering eyes pierced Abracadabra. "You know something of this cursed relationship, I think."

Abracadabra nodded silently.

"There is one piece of advice I *can* give you."

"Please."

"Remember your will."

"You mean my magical will?"

Aleister nodded.

"Do what thou wilt shall be the whole of the law," Therion said, though he sounded like he was parroting in mockery. *"A crock of shit!"*

Aleister sighed.

"Your will, Abracadabra, is the will of the universe. It has to be. How else could you have come so far and done so much? My whole life I searched for the Promised Child, Horus reborn, who would begin the new eon. There were many false prophets. I could not see clearly . . . "

"Aren't you Horus?"

Again that monosyllabic laugh.

"Horus the elder perhaps. Not the *true* Horus. But you . . . you could be."

"You all seem to know a lot more about me than I know of you," Abracadabra said.

"We have watched you from afar," Aleister said. "We have been with you in all your trials and tribulations. At times, you have heard our voices. Not just us three, but others too. Every action has an equal and opposite reaction, that is how the scientists crudely put it, but there is truth in this. Cali's actions have created that equal and opposite reaction, and that is you. Or rather, the *new* you. Some would say that forgetting your true name and nature was a terrible tragedy, and perhaps it was." Aleister's eyes twinkled. "But we must also consider that if you had not, then perhaps Cali would have done away with you from the first—she would have known that the destruction of your physical body would not be enough—and perhaps there would be no hope for Carcosa, as there is now. Her cruelty and malice have made a dream into a man, and a man into a dream. That dream is still within reach. You need only touch it, as you once did The Claw . . . "

They came to the edge of trees. Beyond them lay grasslands stretching to the horizon, though it was barely visible, for the night sky above was increasingly devoid of stars, the lights of heaven winking out as though a black curtain were being drawn across the sky.

All of a sudden, a terrible thunder rumbled, though there were no storm clouds overhead, and deeper beneath the sound—which reminded Abracadabra of the groaning of tectonic plates—was another, that of a hideous, coagulate musical note, a chord that never should have been made, a blasphemy of notes held together by malignant will. His hairs stood on end and his eyes stung. His ears rang. The night-song of the garden had ended. Abracadabra glanced behind him saw the birds taking flight in panic. The lights of the garden flickered, as though candles-flames in the wind.

"What was that?"

"The wall has fallen!" Therion cried.

"What wall?"

"The wall of Carcosa," Aleister said. Abracadabra's heart felt as though it had been pierced by a bright sword. His lifeblood seemed to flow out of him, draining him of all vigour. Aleister's expression saddened. "Time has almost run out."

"Am I too late?"

Rather than answering, the old double-selfed magician stepped from the shadow of the trees and walked onto the grassland, facing the horizon, which now had gained a new definition, the faint outline of deep, spectacular crimson. The very lifeblood Abracadabra had earlier lost now seemed to have coloured the sloping hills, revealing the presence of a hidden spirit beyond where mortal eyes could see.

"Light!" Abracadabra cried, joyfully. All was not darkness. Not yet.

The deep crimson welled, expanded, painted the grasslands, advancing with the surety of water running downhill. Now, the colours were changing, warping through gold, yellow, orange, bronze, and purple.

Aleister threw up his hands in the shape of a V, the posture of the sun-worshipper, and turned to face Abracadabra, now framing the glorious dawn, golden rays spearing around and *through* his twin self. The sun lifted its immense mantle from the lip of the horizon, blinding Abracadabra with penetrating beams, warming him through, and sending light dancing once more through the garden—like happy, fleet-footed children at play.

Haloed now, Aleister's selves began to vibrate, man and beast blurring like mist dissolved by heat, leaving in their place a strange concatenation of the two, a lord bestriding two worlds, a darkness enclosed by light and light enclosed by bright darkness. His form shone, turned translucent by the heliacal rays, seeming as molten honey, a foaming gold without end, eternally renewed.

"Lo!" Aleister cried. "Look to the east, where the All-Conquering Child rises once again!"

With a blast, as though the sun had fired a great flaming arrow into the heart of his being, Abracadabra understood all, and the tears that scalded his cheeks were tears of transcendental joy, tears that were as much fire as his kindled soul, the very essence of him transformed into a divine pyre that knew only a love of the stars.

"I shall not forget your teachings, Aleister! I shall not forget! Thank you!"

Aleister smiled a smile of deepest mystery.

"Do what thou wilt."

He vanished, like the dew of morning in the light of dawn.

CHAPTER 14
THE FLESH IS WEAK

GRIL'DAKKEN CAME AT her with the fury of a dragon wearing human skin, a silent, reptilian killer, his battle-scarred flesh reminding Cali of the many monsters she had hunted in Yhtill during her reckless youth. Those prehistoric monsters only hardened and calcified with age, rather than growing weaker. One could find the shards of old weapons— dagger-tips and arrowheads—imbedded in their scaled flesh, becoming part of their scabrous armour. Gril'dakken was the same.

Cali laughed as he charged, admiring the rippling musculature of his body, moving like clouds in a thunderhead.

"Satan! Kill!"

Her steed leapt forward, jaws flashing. Gril'dakken dodged to the side, the speed at which he could change direction startling. Cali sliced at him with her blade, but the Cannibal King ducked under her weapon. He was freakishly fast for one so large and muscular. She knew then she mustn't underestimate him.

She pulled on Satan's reins, turning the beast. She felt Satan's bristling, kinetic energy, like a loaded spring. He longed to sink his jaws into the saturnine warrior, to devour the devourer.

Cali had trained extensively from the back of a steed, but it was not her preferred way of fighting. Whatever beast she mounted could not move with her balletic grace and precision, and no amount of power compensated for that speed.

Gril'dakken was airborne by the time she had come fully around, his right hand rising to deliver a stunning blow. His face was a kind of tempered savagery—a wild rose garden about to break its bounds. Madness lived only in the eyes, the rest of his porcelain face sculpted into a statuesque neutrality.

84

Cali raised her hand.

"Ka!"

The scream that tore from her throat created a burst of magical force. The Cannibal King was blasted backward. He slammed to the ground, carving a furrow.

But the fight was far from over. Rolling backward, Gril'dakken regained his feet with monkey-like dexterity. Baring bloody, putrid teeth, he charged again.

Cali kicked Satan's flanks, and the gorgonopsid barrelled forward.

He will dodge again, she thought. *And then my blade will be ready for him.*

Gril'dakken came on, a headlong charge, like the wrath of the bleak constellation of Taurus itself.

The gorgonopsid let out a savage snarl.

Cali realised her mistake too late. Her steed, Satan, slammed with all his unbridled fury into Gril'dakken, foreclaws tearing, teeth snapping.

But the Cannibal King had met the charge head on.

His gigantic arms wrapped about the beast's neck, as though hugging the gorgonopsid to his breast. Satan's head was trapped over the giant's shoulder, snapping uselessly at air. Satan raked great gouges in Gril'dakken's chest; blood ran freely, daubing him in a new heraldry, but it seemed the warrior king cared naught.

He cannot, surely he cannot . . . Cali hated the taste of fear that had arisen in her mouth, for Gril'dakken was tightening his grip, his muscles bulging, straining as though about to rip apart the prison of his flesh. She raised her sword to deliver a fatal blow, but then lost her aim as Gril'dakken lifted both Satan and her clean from the ground. Terror filled her heart as she beheld his unnatural strength. Had the consumption of flesh truly granted him such powers?

He is like you, a dark, wise voice said within her. *A zoophage. He has absorbed the strength of those he has devoured. You must beware him!*

Satan scrabbled manically, legs kicking at air and scoring new cuts in Gril'dakken's flesh; the beast was wild-eyed, disbelieving, confused. It no longer resembled the cunning alpha of its species, but rather a panicked dog in the grip of a mighty gorilla.

Cali raised her other hand, intent upon unleashing another

magic blast, but she could hardly summon the power. Airborne, she could not ground herself; she was vulnerable.

Gril'dakken bent backward, the weight nearly buckling him. Then, with strength like that of an Olympic god, he twisted, hurling both Satan and Cali to the ground with meteoric force. Cali's reflexes were lightning; she leapt from her steed's back, somersaulting through the air to land a few feet away. Satan was not so agile, still trapped in the giant's terrible grip. Gril'dakken brought the beast slamming to the earth. Satan's abnormal weight and size at last proved a disadvantage, the impact cracked ribs and bent one leg backwards with a sickening *snap*; the gorgonopsid let out a draconian hiss that was moments later strangled as Gril'dakken tightened his arms about the creature's neck once more.

Cali raised her hand, summoning forth magic again, but surprise had disorientated her, and she did not want to kill her own steed. The result was the same, however. Gril'dakken twisted with all his superhuman strength. A *crack* louder than thunder sounded, as though the walls of Carcosa had broken a second time, and then the gorgonopsid lay still—or almost still. Satan's corpse twitched like a beached fish in the warrior's death-grip. The mightiest alpha—Pe'kar's favourite—was no more.

Gril'dakken discarded the corpse as one might an empty skin of water. The cannibal's eyes burned with a ferocious lustre, ritual flame fled by the blood of babes. Had he not taken her favourite pet from her, Cali might have been inclined to fantasise about those eyes upon her while the two were locked in rapacious acts of lust, perhaps each devouring the other, taking bites of flesh, baptising their carnality with gore . . . But he had awoken yet deeper channels of rage within her.

"That was a grave mistake," she hissed.

Gril'dakken cocked his head. Against all odds the pale giant grinned, a dark humour surfacing, so alien upon the face of one who feasted on flesh.

"I have never heard you speak," Cali said. "In all the eons that you skulked through my city. But I promise you *will* scream."

The Cannibal King's mouth opened, and for a moment Cali thought he might speak, but then a gurgling sound emerged, a slow staccato that made her think of pebbles being churned in a cauldron.

Laughing, he's laughing!

She was tired of dancing. If she could level a city, then she could break a single man.

She cast aside her sword and raised both hands. Her teeth clamped together in the snarl of a Hyrcan tiger. She brought her hands down and a scream left her lips that caused thunder to ripple across the sky. Rain fell in spitting showers, but it was more like acid, hissing as it struck the ground. Tremors snaked through the earth. Fissures appeared, sand escaping into the depths. The air itself seemed to kinetically detonate. The sand beneath Gril'dakken's feet turned into tiny flames that blasted upward. The elements were colliding, at war with one another. Air, water, fire, and earth all intermixed.

And through the chaos walked the Cannibal King. As the flames licked at him, and the acid rain poured upon his head, causing hissing steam to rise from his scalded flesh, she saw that his hand was moving across his chest, using the blood to daub sigils of protection. So the brute knew a little magic, too? How quaint.

Cali raised her hand, and her sword flashed back to her grip. As she caught it, she leapt forward, slicing with as much force and speed as she could.

A titan's hand caught her at the forearm, and for a moment she was paralysed, stupefied even. She had expected some form of defence, but he had arrested the motion of her blade with effortless ease. *I have no equal. This is impossible.*

Her face was still contorted in a look of utter incredulity as Gril'dakken disarmed her of her blade, taking the sword from her grip with a single chopping motion that bent her wrist back on itself, nearly breaking it. She slammed her knee as hard as she could into Gril'dakken's torso, but found it was like striking an adamantine wall. She screamed in frustration.

"Why!" she snarled. "Why won't you fall?"

She had toppled a city, slain a god; how could this flesh-eating monster possibly stand up to her?

Because you and he are too alike, the dark, guiding voice said. *Because he, too, is a devourer of life.*

The Cannibal King leaned in close to her. She tasted his festering breath, smelled the rot of his teeth, saw up close the strands of meat clinging to the black diamonds set in his gums. Would he sink those teeth into her flesh after he had killed her?

THE KING OF CARCOSA

Would he, of all beings, claim the throne of Carcosa? That would be a grim irony indeed, that neither of Hastur's daughters would ascend, merely some corpse-eater, some animal in human shape.

Cali gritted her teeth. Again she struck him, kicking with all the force she could muster. Metal might have bent beneath her strength. An ordinary man's ribs would have shattered. But it seemed she only bruised him. The Cannibal King grinned. His sickeningly slow laugh sounded again. She slammed her forehead into his face. She reeled, dizzy now, nauseous. Still, his implacable grip held her, so tight she was losing bloodflow to her fingers.

Impossible. Impossible. Her mind was so fixated on the unlikely turn of events she could hardly think of a solution; all her strategies and planning and magic had abandoned her.

But there was one spell. One that had saved her many times. "Shime—!"

Before she could finish the word, his other hand gripped her throat, squeezing the breath from her, his fingers tighter than iron chains. She spluttered, gasped, all the blood being squeezed to her head. She felt like her skull might pop like an overripe boil if he applied just a little too much pressure. She scratched at him like a trapped cat with her free hand. He lifted her from the ground. Her legs kicked frantically.

Gril'dakken cocked his head again. Then he slammed his own forehead into hers. Her spirit was almost knocked out of the cage of her flesh. She convulsed, foaming at the lips, twitching like Satan had in his death-throes. Blood poured down her face from her shattered nose. One eye felt as though it had been pushed deeper into her skull. Her mouth was full of gore, her lips split asunder.

He threw her to the ground and the impact seemed a pleasant bump next to the force of his headbutt.

Flee. Run. The army can kill him. There is no shame . . . no shame in killing this monster by whatever means necessary.

She raised her left hand, opened her mouth to bellow the order to attack. She could hardly see the ranks of her army, however. They seemed miles away.

His fingers once more tightened over her wrist, wrenching her arm upward. Her spine was bent back, and she emitted a squeal for which she felt shame more painful than any of the wounds he had dealt so far.

His other hand came down and gripped her other arm. A foot

planted in her back. He began to pull. *Oh stars, no. No!* She knew what he was going to do, for she had watched him do it to many who crossed the order of cannibals. After her escape from Carcosa's Screaming Pit, she had found the body of a trueborn demon with its wings ripped out in the same manner, one of Pe'kar's great generals laid low, as though they were merely a bug to be played with by a demented toddler.

Panic set in. He was going to rip her arms out of their sockets with raw strength—how could she have ever doubted his power was a match for hers? *Hubris, Cali. Your own nemesis. Hubris!*

At first the pain settled into her joints as they were locked fully taut. A scream tore from her throat. His foot pushed down with a pressure so gradual yet inexorable it was excruciating. She writhed and twisted, but his weight and power pinned her as though the sky itself had toppled. Her right elbow joint clicked, then popped. She screamed again and realised that this was his aim, to put on a show for her soldiers, to dishearten them, to let them know that the Demon Queen was no true god. She could only imagine the confusion in the ranks. She had levelled the walls of Carcosa, which not even Pe'kar had done, yet now she seemed to be losing. She did not wonder at their consternation. She herself could not believe what was happening, though the mounting excruciation was a constant reminder of its reality.

The pressure built in her shoulder joint, along with pain at the elbow as the bones were drawn further apart, ligaments stretching, reached torturous levels.

A sudden crushing force slammed into her elbow—Gril'dakken's other foot. She howled. Sobbed like a little girl, then spasmed, trying to escape his clutches, pride forgotten. He did not relent one inch. Again the foot slammed into her shattered joint, and whatever last dregs of integrity had remained in the structure were destroyed.

He mercilessly reapplied pressure. Now her skin felt like it was stretching.

No, she thought. *No . . . the rite of shimen'nehah . . . I weakened my flesh.*

It was as though Gril'dakken knew all her secrets. How could he? They had never spoken. Did he smell weakness? Perhaps. He seemed more beast than man, anyway.

All thoughts abandoned her as the elbow began to tear. She

squealed like a babe, face screwed up. The pressure—which she had thought ungodly—mounted yet again, a final surge of effort, and with that her joint fully unknotted, as did her pulpy skin, removed and replaced one too many times with the dark magics taught to her by the Demon King. The flesh tearing sounded not unlike fabric shearing away from a piece of cloth; blood sprayed and then welled, gurgling from torn arteries.

Gril'dakken twisted and then ripped her arm free, the forearm coming away from the elbow with a wet, grinding sound. Only a ragged stump remained—all latticework veins and jagged meat with a smooth nub of bone protruding from the gory mess.

In the spray of blood, her spine and left arm were slicked. She had one chance to escape, and this was it. She slipped free, rose, and ran—blindly almost—towards the ranks of her army. She did not hear Gril'dakken pursuing. Instead, she heard the sound of his teeth sinking into the flesh of her arm. She did not know how much of her power that might impart to him, but even a little was too much.

"Attack!" she screamed. "Kill him!"

But her army remained motionless. The Calians looked to one another with shrouded expressions, their hearts closed to her. The trueborns circling overhead looked down with loathing.

Cali trembled, clutching her bleeding stump, uselessly trying to stem the flow of blood. She knew healing magics, but it would take colossal effort and time to heal such a wound, and she had neither. Her army was about to turn on her.

"Please!" She knew as soon as she uttered the word it was folly. The eyes of her followers became hard diamonds.

Oh now you have truly lost them, dear queen, the dark voice said. She had thought of this voice as her own, but now she recognised it as distinct, coming from somewhere outside of herself, addressing her as its recipient. *Now you have only one hope. Me.*

Was she losing her grip of reality? Hallucinating, due to bloodloss?

No. I am real. Realer than you.

"But who are you?" she whispered.

You know. You have always known. I am the last piece of him that remains.

Chills ran through her.

The eyes of thousands judged her next move, but all of a sudden they did not exist. Even Gril'dakken, who now advanced slowly and fearlessly towards her army, aiming to finish what he had started, his mouth crimson with her lifeblood, seemed merely a phantom. The only reality before her was this voice, guiding her.

"Stand aside!" she snarled, and clearly something of her old authority had returned, for the ranks of the army parted in dismay. She lumbered like a drunkard into their midst. She was not fleeing. No, she was *searching*. She had to find it, the source of the voice.

A little farther, a little farther!

And there it was, nestled in a defensive perimeter, guarded by her elite: the black ark forged from pure indignite. The sarcophagus that should have housed Alan Chambers' body, but instead housed something altogether darker.

She staggered towards the ark, and her soldiers all fled, scrabbling backward in the wake of her passage, save for one, who stood his ground like the last watchmen of Ragnarök. Cali left a trail of gore in her wake as she limped toward the cask, her black skin turning ashen with bloodloss. Her eyes, however, gleamed like starry citrine, their light renewed.

"My queen, perhaps you should reconsider . . . "

She struck the objecting soldier with her good hand, and his neck snapped. He fell, instantly dead. No wonder she'd believed herself so powerful: all her servants were weak. She was surrounded by infants. The strong had died in the civil war and past battles with Carcosa. No wonder Pe'kar had been unwilling to attack. He saw the disease at the heart of his nation.

But she could set it right. She had the tool. And more importantly, she had the will.

"I unbind thee, sealing spell," she whispered. The ark glowed briefly, a gleam as though flame-light were reflected in a great mirror-wall of jetstone, and then the light died out. She placed her left hand on the ark (careless now of how her stump bled), finding it cool to the touch like rain-washed granite, and tore the stone lid off the great ornate container.

Yes! Yes! Yes! Come to me! Wield me! I am yours!

Within the pit of the ark, shrouded in a shadow that seemed of its own making, was the talisman forged in the Fires of Manifestation by the Demon King; his masterwork, never to be replicated or equalled; the great, cursed object that once had been wielded by her mortal foe, Alan Chambers.

The Claw.

It looked different to when she had cut it from Alan's hand. Parts seemed to have been added, as though it had grown in the dank confines of the ark like a hidden fungus. It now sported a gleaming, plated forearm and the intricate pieces of an elbow joint. Its surface was chrome yet scaly, as though a great lizard had been skinned, its leathern flesh stretched over machinelike contraptions. Oils flowed through tubes that could have been real arteries, or could have been simulacrums. Its talons winked like dragon's teeth. *It has remade itself for me,* she thought, both gladness and sickening fear coursing through her bloodstream. *It knows. It wants me.*

I want one to wield me who has the strength to do what is necessary, The Claw answered. *I want you to harness my full power. Bring the city to its knees. Become the Black Empress!*

Even now, half-dead, her life spilling onto the sand with every second, she hesitated. Once she donned The Claw, there was no turning back. This was a pact made unto eternity.

Perhaps it is better to die here, she thought. *Better to fail.*

No.

Perhaps The Claw answered her, or perhaps it was another voice deep within her; she could no longer tell the difference.

She reached in and took The Claw. With a cry that sounded like triumph mixed with bottomless grief, she brought the profane artefact to her grisly wound, and felt the first penetration—almost sexual—as its dreadful mechanisms activated, soldering not just to her flesh but to her soul.

CHAPTER 15
HOW THE MIGHTY HAVE FALLEN

"**O**CALI, WHAT have you done?" Cassilda whispered. From the rubble of her city walls, surrounded by what little remained of the Carcosan infantry, Cassilda witnessed Cali's desperate act. Terror, awe, pity, grief, despair, and anger all warred within her as she saw her sister bind herself to The Claw, heard the screams as its cursed matter infiltrated her being, saw the terrible delight in her eyes as the transformation was complete.

Cali raised the gleaming weapon into the air, a symbol of utter dominion—at the heaviest of all prices. Despite her hatred of The Claw, Cassilda could not help but think of it as part of Alan, and that in wearing it, Cali was now desecrating her lover's corpse.

Yellow light blazed from Cali, rocketing up into the sky, forming a baleful pillar that seemed to shine with the same iridescence as the King In Yellow's secret eyes. The pillar writhed and zagged like a dancing serpent, then exploded, illuminating the vast, numberless host at Cali's beck and call. Whatever loyalty they'd lost had been restored to them, for now they all gave a salute—a motion like slicing the wrist and raising their finger to the sky—bellowing Cali's name to the heavens as though she were the Creator incarnated.

If my father could see this now . . . Cassilda could hardly finish the thought. Such was the bleak ruin of all their hopes that thinking was almost impossible.

"So she has made her final pact, crossed her final threshold," Petruccio said, grimly.

"But she does it not to defend others, like Alan," LeBarron said. "But to advantage herself. It will go even more bleakly for her than for Alan and Haercus. The madness will rot her like a cancer."

93

THE KING OF CARCOSA

"I doubt we will be around to witness her inglorious decline," Petruccio replied wryly. Certain death had made him strangely glib, as though life were indeed a joke after all, and he would be glad when it reached the cosmic punchline of his own end.

"Gril'dakken may still stand a chance," LeBarron said.

Petruccio made a grunting noise and said nothing.

Cali marched out from the ranks of her army, who were now forming up upon her, like detritus carried in the wake of a large cruising ship, the waves of her passage creating a slipstream of energy that was not only physical but spiritual too, their hearts aligning with hers, their minds bent beneath the resurgence of her will. Gril'dakken stood his ground, dauntless to the very last, but as he moved to intercept Cali she raised The Claw and a blast of light near blinded Cassilda. When she had blinked away stars, the Cannibal King was no more—not even dust remained.

"By the Black Star," LeBarron hissed. "Woe indeed."

"We can't hold her here. Flee back to the palace," Petruccio said. "All withdraw!"

The orders were related. Cassilda, Petruccio, and LeBarron fled with their soldiers.

As she ran, Cassilda found she hardly recognised the streets of her own city. For one thing, they were still. The once ever-shifting landscape of Carcosa had been frozen, as though the city were in reality a small mammal that had caught sight of a great predator. Perhaps the unspelling of the walls had uprooted some deep-seated magic of the city. Perhaps the city was laying its belly open, offering its throat to the one it knew would win. Whatever the case, the transformation that had so animated the organic substance of Carcosa was now dormant, its spires more like fossils stuck into deadened earth, its strangely arterial roads no more than ossuaries.

Through desolate market stalls and empty alleyways, they ran like scared children.

Winged shadows gathered overhead.

And then the trueborns swooped down upon the trio.

They fought, but it was without heart. Petruccio raised his hand and sent great sheets of flame at the winged demons. LeBarron's sword flashed to and fro, duelling a cunning opponent. Cassilda sent blades of sound through the hearts of her enemies. But all felt vain, hopeless. Any they killed were replaced by two more. The

94

hydra of Cali's army would win through belligerence, let alone her newfound powers.

A shining, purple-fleshed demon descended upon Cassilda. She emitted a high, piercing note and magic left her fingertips, causing the air to ripple and distort with its passage. But the demon was agile as a cat, twisting and diving, avoiding the passage of her spell, landing before her with balletic poise.

His mouth was a cruel glimmer of needle-teeth as he smiled. His cone-shaped head was as much a blade as the serpent-wave dagger in his hand—a many-thonged whip dangled from the other.

Strangely, the demon bowed before Cassilda.

"Is this mockery?" Cassilda spat.

"No," the trueborn said. "This is honour. My name is Malebolge, whom my enemies call 'The Cruel'. One of three brothers." He pointed with his dagger at where another trueborn, with lilac-coloured skin and wielding a long rapier, fought LeBarron. "That is De'kata, the Relentless. And there, fighting your little friend, Ashe'oken, the Unparalleled."

"Are all Pe'karians egomaniacs?"

Malebolge chuckled.

"We are Calians now. And yes, in a way. Honour, title, recognition, that is what we crave. Your lives seem quotidian to us, Carcosan. But hush, I speak with disrespect to one who is a princess." His smile widened and widened, revealing more teeth than Cassilda would have thought possible. "And to kill you will be a glory that will finally set me above my kin!"

He wasted no further time. The whip cracked. Cassilda could not have moved fast enough to evade it even had she been as skilful a fighter as her sister. The barbed thongs wrapped around her leg, biting deep. Blood welled, and the demon dragged her shrieking to the ground. She reached down for the knife she normally kept at her thigh but found it missing. Somewhere on her long journey she had evidently misplaced it, perhaps in the battle at Pe'kar's court. She cursed herself for such a careless oversight.

You wasted a visit to the vaults, she thought. *There would have been ample weapons there.*

Malebolge looped the whip around his forearm and began to pull, dragging her along the ground toward him. Cassilda raised her hand, uttering monosyllabic song-words, each one producing projectiles of shimmering non-being, blades invisible save for the way they scarred the air itself; the demon dodged, laughing.

But she had not been aiming at him.

The whip in his hand was sliced as easily as a single thread of yarn. She rose. Malebolge was airborne, having taken the skies to avoid her missiles, and swooped around for another attack, his dagger in hand, flashing like the premonition of a thunderbolt.

Cassilda screamed, and the shockwave cracked the walls of the buildings on either side, caused the fights taking place around her to momentarily halt; Carcosan soldiers, seeing who it was who'd uttered the cry, took heart and renewed their frantic defences, though they were hopelessly outnumbered and outmanoeuvred by their winged enemies.

Malebolge tumbled, knocked out of flight. But he had not been flying high and landed with little injury. Getting to his feet, she saw his grin had at last been transformed into a grimace, blood leaking from a gash in his face, anger burning in his eyes.

"I shall present you as a coat of flesh to Cali," Malebolge snarled.

"You shall bore me to death," Cassilda replied.

Malebolge screamed, hurling himself at Cassilda—precisely what she wanted. Using the very last depths of her lungs, she summoned a note of piercing shrillness, as lethal and disturbing as poison dripped into a dreamer's sleeping ear. Malebolge's wings ceased working mid-flight, a form of paralysis taking hold of his limbs with greater binding power than lead chains. The knife dropped from his hand, and he collapsed like a boneless fish upon the pavement.

She had no magic left in her. So she would end this another way. Cassilda picked up a heavy stone, part of the rubble of the city, and held it high over her head. The weight caused her to sway a little. That, and the blood loss of her leg wound. She gritted her teeth. She was sure to die this day, but not to this cretin.

She brought the stone down as hard as she could on Malebolge's head.

The elongated skull split like an eggshell, spilling pink yoke across the streets of Carcosa. There was a grim satisfaction in that, as though she had made an offering to the city.

She let out a breath, woozy and exhausted. She had to find LeBarron and Petruccio, continue leading the retreat.

As she turned away, Malebolge's corpse surged upward one final time. She wheeled around, but not fast enough to prevent the teeth of his hideous mouth clamping down upon her thigh.

She screamed. The needles were razor sharp, cutting through flesh, muscle, and tendon with ease, perforating even the bone beneath. She stared down in horror at the cracked and leaking cavity of Malebolge's now concave skull. There were no eyes or nose left. The skull had been made into a bowl filled with grey, pink, and red soup. Yet, the mouth seemed to have a life of its own, chewing upon the meat of her leg in an autonomic function.

She collapsed to the ground, still screaming. The pain was excruciating. She imagined his fangs had to be coated with some kind of venom, for no simple stab wound could hurt so much.

Summoning internal strength, she raised her free leg and kicked. Malebolge's body twitched. His teeth remained lodged in her flesh. The agony almost sent her reeling into blackness, but she knew if she fell unconscious now, then all truly would be lost. She kicked again. Then again. With each kick, his teeth loosened. Some broke off, remaining imbedded in her thigh like marrow-coloured darts. Others shattered and fell away. Blood welled and welled. Great mouthfuls of flesh were torn, revealing ragged edges of bloodied musculature. Her skin—partially peeled back by the action of the demon's teeth—looked fake, almost, like the tissue fabricated by a magician to cloak an automaton.

With one last kick, Malebolge fell away. If he had been alive when he bit her, he was dead now. Perhaps his final act had simply been an involuntarily action, muscle-memory. Dogs, after all, could still lock their jaws even in death, and hornets still use their stingers. *And that is all you are, a beast,* she thought, savagely. *For all your pride and ego, just a beast.*

She made to stand, but could not. The wound was not mere surface graze, but had destroyed ligaments and muscle-connections of her leg. She rolled onto her front, and squealed as she felt pieces of her falling out of place, the blood running even more eagerly.

Drag yourself. Drag. Come on!

She crawled on all fours. She could see light ahead—Petruccio's glorious armour. The dwarf had just put an end to his own foe. LeBarron was somewhere nearby, but she couldn't see him.

"Petruccio!" Cassilda cried.

The dwarf turned. His eyes widened, and he came hurrying toward her, but the way was not easy. Demons circled overhead. Countless dead Carcosan soldiers lay strewn across the street.

THE KING OF CARCOSA

Living Carcosans were running in panic, stampeding over the recent battlefield, fleeing before Cali's approaching army. If they saw their princess in plight, they cared not, running past her, some even treading on her in their haste to reach the palace—little good it would do them.

It's all over. Carcosa is already dead. We are not a people anymore. They do not know me, and I do not know them. The hour of wolves is upon us. Cali has won.

Black thoughts consumed her, to the point she was almost ready to lie down among the dead and simply wait to be trodden into the ground, reduced to bloody paste, by the very people she'd sworn to defend.

Petruccio suddenly halted, his eyes tearing away from her and looking upward. Cassilda looked over her shoulder, following his gaze. Her heart felt as though it was seized by a dark hand.

From the spire of a looming church building, one whose bells had at long last ceased tolling, stood Cali. Though she was smeared in blood and bore many injuries, Cassilda had to admit that the Black Empress was worthy of her name. Indeed, Cassilda no longer recognised her sister. The coal-fleshed eidolon who looked down on her could never have once been a little girl; she must have sprung fully-formed from the void.

Silver chains connected choicely placed pieces of aureate armour. From her belt hung the crooked harp that had brought Carcosa's walls to the ground. Her head was crowned with a tiara of thorny indignite. In one hand, she held a glittering, curved blade. Her other was the talisman once worn by the man Cassilda loved, the glowing hand with which one could grip the slippery thing called reality itself, though to do so incurred the most terrible price, for it could not be done sanely.

Cassilda waited what felt like an age for Cali to speak, but the languorous goddess did not deign to offer her even parting words. Instead, Cali turned her yellow orbs upon another viridian spire, rising opposite her with the insane ambition of a skyscraper clawing the heavens. Golgon, the church was called. Cassilda remembered the day it had been consecrated by her father, sanctified for the purpose of religious devotion, its vacancy filled by the waters of meaning. She doubted Cali recalled such an occasion. She had been too busy strengthening her sword-arm and exploring other worlds for such ceremonies.

Raising The Claw, Cali flicked her wrist just once, and five beams of light shot from the ends of her metallic fingertips. With a noise like stone churned in the mouth of a titan-worm, the light sliced through the building as though it were no more substantial than a mirage. Golgon groaned, cracks forming across its ancient, mossy edifice, dust and pebble-rain crumbling away from the wounds like expelled breath. As though a winded drunkard, Golgon swayed, then began to lean, its shadow falling across Cassilda as she realised with horror what her sister intended.

She will not even kill me directly, Cassilda thought. And she knew it was no sisterly affection that held Cali back, merely economy. With this, Cali would kill three enemies with one stone—quite literally.

Golgon tumbled, shedding stones and rubble even as it fell, its scars breaking and spitting detritus. Its proud head, which had once grazed the clouds, now hurtled down with the inevitability of a suicidal jumper. With dark irony, the falling motion caused Golgon's bell to toll one final time, a knell that seemed to shimmer in the air like a prophet's vision. The brightness of the note was a terror to Cassilda, the chord of her own unmaking, and the unmaking of Carcosa itself. If Cali's dreadful harp had sounded the overture, then this bell's resonance was the final, funereal coda.

Or would have been, if not for Petruccio.

The dwarf stood over Cassilda and raised his hands to the heavens, which were now blotted out entirely by the chthonic swordblade of the crumbling tower. From his lips spilled a gurgle of magical song, a sibilance of notes at once guttural and harsh, yet in their combination oddly beautiful. His face was more set than any she had ever seen, more fixed than the constellations that mapped the skies. His eyes shone brighter than even his armour, a purer diamond still.

Cassilda's mouth opened wide in awe as the power of Petruccio's spell rippled out from him, a shuddering wind that snapped at her hair and raised goosebumps upon her arm. A tornado of raw force cloaked him. His howling voice rose like the lament of the damned.

The tower, still groaning in its ruinous descent, began to slow. And then, it *stopped.*

Cassilda blinked, astonished and bewildered. The dwarf had frozen the tower mid-fall. But how? What kind of magic could lift such a titanic weight? She knew of spells of flight, spells of prodigious force, but nothing that could freeze an object of such colossal proportions in motion. Why, if she had known such magic, she might have lifted the Siege Ender during the battle of Carcosa and thrown it back into the desert from whence it came, or at very least stopped it at the walls.

Petruccio's every limb trembled with the exertion. Blood ran from his nose. The ground beneath his feet cracked as his armour-shod feet were driven by the churchspire's weight into the ground.

And that is when she realised what he had done. He was not holding the tower with magic, he was merely using magic to extend his reach.

Petruccio held the tower with his own physical strength.

"Take her, LeBarron!" Petruccio screamed. His vocal chords sounded like they might burst. Veins and tendons rose to the surface of his face that had no right to be seen. His arms shook so violently she thought they might soon produce flame.

Cassilda felt arms about her, the mummer lifting her to her feet. He was covered in blood, mud, and dust. He looked like a zombie who had dug their way out of a fresh grave. His strong arms held her upright, supporting her ravaged leg.

"I have you princess," LeBarron whispered.

"Go!" Petruccio screamed.

LeBarron dragged Cassilda away.

"Wait . . . we can't . . . we mustn't . . . " Bloodloss had made her weak, confused. They couldn't leave Petruccio, but that's exactly what they were doing; LeBarron half carried her out from under the tower's guillotine. Carcosan soldiers fled with them, escaping the trap like ants scurrying out from beneath the looming shadow of a raised boot.

Cassilda turned her gaze toward Cali, who still stood upon her own spire, a terrible smile forming on her glowing face as she looked down at the tiny figure, perhaps the smallest soul in all Carcosa, who yet defied all her awesome might.

No, Cassilda thought. *He is a giant. A god. See how he shines!*

"Impressive," Cali said, and the word—though not shouted—somehow resonated enough to be heard across the entire city. "But it is over, Petruccio."

Cali flicked her wrist, and the tower's stasis was unmade, the full weight of the sky-rending spire falling upon Petruccio with the thunder of God's hammer.

CHAPTER 16
THE FATHER, THE SON, AND THE SERPENT

T HE SUN'S BLISTERING rays continued to illuminate the garden. Abracadabra found his heart lifting and lifting, as though borne upon the winds of strange joy. But the miracle was not ended; in fact, it had only just begun.

Now, framed in the sun's yellow light, he saw the shadow of a man—no, something greater than a man. It was as though the light were indeed liquid, a cauldron of yellow ichor, and from this soup limbs and form were developing, like a babe in the amniotic fluid of the womb. If this process went on for hours or even days, Abracadabra did not know, for he remained transfixed. And where usually one's eyes might be burned out by sunlight, he found he could continue to stare without harm, ensorcelled by the process he bore witness to.

The cauldron of yellow liquid tipped, or rather was punctured, releasing a dram of golden-bright liquid. The fluid poured out onto the hilltop, as though the distance between celestial body and ground were merely a few hundred feet and not thousands of miles. *But in this place, all distances are near, and all nearnesses are far*, Abracadabra thought. Such was the divine mystery.

Sluicing down in the embrace of the xanthous waters was a tall, beauteous form. In a plash of yellow sludge, it landed upon the hill's crown and lay motionless. Then slowly, this figure began to rise, newborn and yet perfectly formed, filthy with the mud of creation and yet spotless in every way, an Adam in the first days of the Eden.

Abracadabra realised he looked upon the naked form of The King In Yellow.

THE KING OF CARCOSA

Prostrate, weeping, he abased himself before the godlike being. Slowly, The King made his way towards him.

"O, my dear Abracadabra, why dost thou kneel?"

"In awe of thy majesty, O Great King."

"Kneel not, for thine is the glory, and thine the majesty," The King said. "The world is thine. And thee, the world."

Abracadabra raised his eyes and beheld a face so beatific his senses were startled. For a moment, his concept of the body faded, and he was among the birds singing, among the branches growing inch by inch over long decades, among the sunlight itself, spearing through the canopies, among the creeping caterpillars and the weaving spiders, and then he was back, still paralysed by the beauty, hypnotised like a serpent by the sweet music of a pipe.

The King extended a hand. Abracadabra took it and rose.

"It is time for thee to meet my maker—and thine."

The King took Abracadabra back into the garden, leading him on a pathway with no name nor mapped route, until they reached what Abracadabra knew—though he did know *how* he knew—was the very centre.

There was a glade, the edge of which he stood at, only glimpsing what lay beyond a circle of closely cropped trees—flashes of iridescent colour, as though at long last he had found rainbow's end.

"I'm scared."

"As thou shouldst be," The King whispered. "It is a fearful thing, to fall into the hands of the living God. But that is what thou must do. I will be with thee."

Abracadabra nodded. Then, with a motion that felt ageless in the execution, he stepped through the trees and into the centre.

A tree grew, of nameless species, though Abracadabra thought he knew of one counterpart to its infernal majesty: the tree he'd encountered in Pe'kar's courtroom. In any other instance, the tree might have commanded his entire attention: the way its spiked branches seemed to form a crown of thorns, the way its glossy bark seemed to swallow light and present mirages upon its surface, shadows familiar and strange, or the way its boughs were crowned with laurels of ten thousand varieties of flower, each more alien and exotic than the last, as though in this tree's fecundity lived the archetype of every known being.

But the tree was naught compared to that which encoiled it: a great serpent the like of which Abracadabra had never seen.

From the peak of the tree—which disappeared beyond where Alan's eyes could see, some heaven-gate that opened upon infinity—it descended, wrapping about the tree with its massy coils. Its scales were every colour of the rainbow, a hallucinogenic warping of colour that shimmered and danced in patterns knowing no beginning nor end. Such was the intensity of the colours that Abracadabra felt he could *hear* them, a song forming in the back of his brain as oranges morphed into blues, yellows into greens, purples into the deepest crimson, a language without words, a language of pure and indescribable beauty. No acid trip or DMT quest could equal the sensory stimulation—it left him dumbstruck, drooling almost. Every slightest permutation of the vision evoked in him vast analogs of experience, as though his mind were a library, and with each new colour he opened a new book, a vellum tome binding thousands upon thousands of pages, and drank of a life he had never known. Centuries passed in each microcosmic second.

With agony, he forced himself to look at the serpent's face, knowing he was unworthy of such a vision, but knowing also that he could only now go forward, that to turn back from the precipice of this final unfurling were impossible. He found—somewhat with surprise—the serpent's eyes were not directed at him. This led Abracadabra to take in the final strangeness of the scene before him.

A man knelt, tending the serpent, tenderness in his every movement like one on the brink of marriage proposal. The Great Serpent regarded him in turn with unblinking adoration, their mutual fixation seeming to encompass the entirety of existence, every polarity resolved in their unbroken yet unconsummated fascination: beast and man, male and female, brightness and darkness, hardness and softness. Theirs was the interplay of all-yin and all-yang in the ceaseless action of the universe—an action that could only be described as *love*.

For all the cosmic portents of the scene, Abracadabra noticed sundry details as well. The man was dark of skin, with curly black hair thick as bristles. In many ways, he looked like Abracadabra himself . . . And all at once, Abracadabra recognised the man.

"Father?"

Uboth turned from his immortal duty of tending the serpent and smiled.

"Did I not tell you all things spin upon the dragon-wheel. And that which is lost returns to us in glory?" Then Uboth grinned, surprisingly boyish despite the age that lived in his eyes. "Good to see you, kid."

Abracadabra smiled and bowed, caught between affection and formality.

"You did tell me, but I did not understand."

"How could you? Here, understanding ceases. It must."

"How long have you been here?"

"A day. A thousand years. There's no difference," Uboth said.

Abracadabra nodded.

"You are the True Serpent, Alan," Uboth said. "And counterpoint to Cali's false one. Very few ever reach this place, a mere handful in fact. You have done so well. But I think you know there is one last thing you must do."

Abracadabra nodded.

His father sighed, sadness in his eyes.

"Come, you must receive the blessing."

At first Abracadabra hesitated, unsure what was required. But Uboth beckoned him softly, and he began to approach. He was not sure how to move, how to walk; should he shuffle forward in a bowing posture, as servants had in the court of the Chinese Emperor? Or should he stride confidently, conveying a sense that he belonged in this kingdom within a kingdom, this sanctuary of sanctuaries.

He knelt by his father, who embraced him briefly. Abracadabra could have wept, but he knew he was about to experience something that would require all his strength to survive, not for its terror, but for its wonder; not for its horror, but for its beauty. Mortal men were not meant to endure such glories—hence why Enoch was raptured by the spirit of God. And though Abracadabra was far from ordinary, he had lived as an ordinary man, and knew the pain of flesh, the burden of time, and the numbing cold of death.

"Look into the eyes," Uboth whispered.

Heart thundering, Abracadabra turned his gaze slowly to meet the adoring serpent, and no sooner had his eyes fixed upon the slitted orbs—in which he saw his own bright reflection—than he was blasted by a force like he had never known, an incandescence that cut through him like the cold of a blizzard, only it was warm,

warm like nothing he could describe, melting away his exterior until all that was left was a throbbing rawness of naked spirit. His memory and past were sloughed like wet paper. His pain was sluiced into a cosmic drain, and what filled him up was a love he could never believe that he could have deserved, even were he to live virtuously a thousand years. The strangest thing was the love was not directed toward him, but *from* him. It was not the compassion of another that moved him, but his own. The devastating force of his own goodness almost caused him to come undone. His every atom hummed with ecstatic realisation of his own pure love. Cassilda, Petruccio, LeBarron, a thousand other names, their faces flashing before him, his spirit enveloping them. The idea that he had a limited supply of love to give seemed ludicrous, laughable. Indeed, the more he loved the more the wellspring overflowed, until the very stars themselves were the objects of his adoration, and his spirit was cast like seed through the invisible body of the cosmos, growing everywhere it was planted.

And then one face loomed before him which—for the briefest moment—he thought he could not love.

Cali.

Her dark radiance was a bane upon his soul, a single note of dissonance in an otherwise celestial symphony. But how foolish was he to doubt, even for a moment! In the serpent's eyes—which had now become *her* eyes—he found only deeper depths of love, and with a cry from his lips like the apex of orgasm he cast his love forth to her, embracing her as he would his own deepest and innermost self, which he knew, in that divine moment, is exactly what she was.

When he had first beheld Carcosa, he had wept. But now he went beyond tears, his very physicality destroyed by the extasis of utter compassion.

"That is enough," a gentle voice said.

And suddenly, it was over. Uboth held him, as though he were but a child again, his face showing a grave understanding of the burden, the near-torment, of such love.

"You did well," he said.

Abracadabra continued to sob, though it was more like bleeding than crying.

"He must return to his duty now, dear Abracadabra." The

THE KING OF CARCOSA

King's voice roused Abracadabra from his delirium. He nodded, thanking Uboth, and embracing his father once more. Then he rose and stepped back. Uboth smiled, then turned his eyes back to the serpent, there to once more complete the eternal loop, the ceaseless interplay of all polarity in the endless dragon-wheel of time. Abracadabra had been part of that loop at its deepest rung for only a moment, but he knew he could never again see the world with the same eyes. Forever he would gaze through the eyes of the Great Serpent, and see all re-clad in the glimmering raiment of eternal compassion.

"In the Great Serpent, all things are renewed," the King said. "Including me . . . "

Abracadabra turned to The King.

"That is how you can come back," he said. "The Serpent can send you back."

Abracadabra was silent for a while, considering what was being offered.

"I have returned upon the wheel many times, dear Abracadabra, but now is the time for me to abandon the wheel entirely. I am old—impossibly old, even by thy reckoning—and the Great Serpent has at last seen fit to free me from this karma."

"I don't understand."

"I shall not return to Carcosa. The King In Yellow is no more." Strangely, the King was smiling at these words. "But thou, thou shalt go in my stead."

Comprehension dawned.

"You sacrifice your divinity for me?"

"No. I shall still be eternal, as all beings are who live in awe of the True Magic, but that eternity shall not be renewed upon the black planet or any other. I shall go forth into the realm of the spirit, into the final mystery, never to return."

Abracadabra wanted to object, but knew objections were pointless.

"I shall miss you," he said.

"And I shall miss thee, dear Abracadabra."

The King smiled, then stepped towards the tree and the Great Serpent encoiling it, like a great strand of glittering DNA about a fulcrum running through the heart of the universe itself.

"I am ready," the King said, quietly.

"Goodbye, old friend," Uboth whispered.

"Goodbye."

The serpent's eyes left Uboth; the mighty snake reared up its head, staring directly into the eyes of The Yellow King. The King extended his hands either side, palms facing forwards, standing in what resembled a yogic mountain-pose, a posture of utter surrender and yet also indomitable pride.

"Thank you," he said.

The serpent struck, fangs flashing like twin thunderbolts, and as they closed about the King's neck, there was a flash of multicoloured light. The King's perfect form became a kaleidoscope, turned inside out, his every atom flashing a contrasting and garish hue, a motley being, as though he were being dressed in the robes of a jester. And then, he became dust, bright rainbow sparkles that floated upward on an invisible current, borne skyward towards the tree's upper boughs. And there, before Abracadabra's astonished eyes, the dust settled upon a branch. For a moment, it remained there, aglitter, and then a flower began to bloom.

It was a xanthimum, but of a hue deeper than any yellow Abracadabra had ever known. Once more, tears scored Abracadabra's face as he watched the bright flower form, a rare and beautiful bloom even among the celestial blossoms of the garden, perhaps even the most beautiful upon the whole tree.

"One day, you shall take your place upon the tree," Uboth said.

Abracadabra turned and saw tears running down his father's face.

"What about you?"

Uboth shook his head.

"Such is the nature of being an artist. In the act of recording, we separate ourselves from the experience. Thus, I am at once infinitely blessed and terribly cursed. This is to be my eternal fate, dwelling at the very seat of God, cherished beyond all beings, and yet outcast from the final mystery." Uboth wiped away his tears. "But I do not weep for myself. I weep for you, dear son."

Abracadabra felt like an axe had cleaved his heart.

"I'm sorry, father. Truly."

"It is not your fault. Nor mine. This is what must happen. You know already, don't you?"

Abracadabra nodded.

"Then step forward. It is time, at last."

THE KING OF CARCOSA

Trembling, Abracadabra stepped before the serpent, once more hypnotised by the mystery indwelling its eternal and unblinking gaze, once more ensnared by the colours of its rainbow scales. Whether Abracadabra stood back to behold its enormous wonder, or zoomed in to examine the smallest scale, he found all was infinitely complex, infinitely beautiful, worlds living even within the ridges that divided scale from scale, layer from layer.

Such was his enchantment that he did not flinch as the serpent's fangs bit down into the crown of his skull, nor as he was lifted from his feet, carried upward into some fathomless darkness that he knew was the darkness of life itself.

CHAPTER 17
THE FIRES DIE

NOW THAT HER greatest enemies lay dead under the rubble, there was nothing to stop Cali. She had fought her way up to the slopes of the palace. Though she had killed many a Carcosan, in truth, she had lost her appetite for wanton slaughter. She was ready to rule, ready to receive the adoration of her people. But first, she knew she must claim the palace. From there, she would establish her mastery of the black planet.

A few mad soldiers who still believed they could save the city stood before her, their eurypterid armour making them look like giant insects. And indeed, that is all they were to Cali. With a single swipe of The Claw, a blast of thunderous energy that resembled yellow lightning, they were rent asunder, reduced to mere body parts and ash.

She fought her way up the steppe, although if truth be told, she little regarded what she was doing as "fighting". The Carcosans were no match for her. Even their most experienced soldiers—of those who had not yet fled the city—died beneath a single blow, their weapons and armour-plating shattered, their faces and limbs rent beyond repair. With almost lazy swipes of her talismanic hand, she removed every obstacle, every gnat buzzing about her ear, until at last she stood before the great pillars. For a second she hesitated, looking down at the base one of the pillars, where a dark stain still marred the stone, an eternal mark upon the palace's visage. *Erik,* she thought. *O Erik. I do regret what happened to thee. You should have had a place in this new world order. You should have been at my side.*

Courtiers poured out of the mouth of the palace, prostrating themselves before her, swearing loyalty and fealty. With a single motion of her hand all were obliterated, their blood washing the palace's colonnaded vestibule. She stepped over their pulpy remained and into the interior.

A few soldiers greeted her, but resistance here was even thinner than she had anticipated. Calian soldiers rushed in behind her and began their pillage and looting. She did not bother to restrain them. They had been coiled springs the entire march; to hold them back at this, the moment of absolute victory, would be like trying to prize a bone out of a rabid dog's jaws. Let them have their slaughter, their looting, their bloodshed, their rape, their pillage, their desecrations. Tomorrow, she might well dispose of them. They were wretched things, beneath her. And she had not forgotten how so many seemed ready to betray her when the fight with Gril'dakken had turned ill.

Guided by some dark intuition, Cali plunged deeper into the palace. She passed her own quarters, and there used The Claw to set all of her old belongings ablaze. She disintegrated the bed. It served only to remind her of former chains, the chains of her desire and addiction and carnality, which she had finally slipped.

For what pleasure lies in pleasure when you have power? The Claw remarked.

Cali smiled.

Wisely observed.

In the corridors outside her quarters, she killed half a dozen more courtiers. A soldier charged her with a spear and she cut him into five ribbons vertically, and watched as the pieces of him fell apart like cuttings of choice steak.

At last, she came to where her intuition had been leading her: a door, seemingly carved of obelisk, though in truth none knew the material from which a demonic door was formed—dreamstuff, perhaps, substance only the oneiric pigment could invent. A chthonian face protruded outward, daring all who approached the door to pay homage to its imposing gravitas. As she stepped nearer, the door's eyes flicked open.

"Hephaiton," she purred.

The great door blinked in acknowledgement.

"It has been a while," she said.

"It has been no time at all in my great span, Princess Cali."

His speech was glacial, like titanic icebergs slowly cleaving apart in the high arctic. "*But I see that you are changed.*"

"Princess no longer," she said. "I am Empress now. The Empress of the black planet."

The door chewed her words.

"*And who proclaimed you empress?*"

"I did," Cali sneered. "All great souls are the authors of their own destiny. Had I waited for Father to pass the crown, I should have waited until the twin suns burned out, and the Black Star itself faded into darkness. I am the Black Empress, Hephaiton. And you will open for me."

The door smiled, revealing needle-teeth.

"*No access is granted to the Fires of Manifestation, save by order of the Yellow King. DEATHLESS BE HE!*"

Cali's smile became lunatic.

"The King In Yellow is dead, you old fool. And he is not coming back."

Hephaiton's face became a mask of sorrow, his brow furrowing, forming trenches in his face.

"*If your words are true, then the door to the Fires shall remain forever shut. I shall remain sealed, never again opening, not even at the ending of the world.*"

"How noble!" Cali spat. "But you *shall* open, old fool. I have endured your patronising tones and your stultifying idiocy long enough." She raised The Claw. Her grin became a Pe'karian rictus. "Open-sesame!"

In the split second before the beam left The Claw, the instance between life and death, over which Cali had near absolute command, the door smiled back at Cali, and with an inhalation of breath so powerful it might have plucked a lesser foe from their feet and sent them sprawling across the ground, the great door bellowed for the last time: "*HAIL TO THE YELLOW KING!*"

Even as the beam of diseased light cut through Hephaiton's ancient frame, blasting his face to smithereens, the doorway's final words rang through the palace, and those fleeing in panic felt the smallest ebb of courage once more fill their hearts—if only for a moment.

But then, the door was silenced forever, its hinges annihilated, its face shattered into a thousand pieces. It was as though Cali had taken an adamantine hammer to the very face of Michaelangelo's

David, laughing as its priceless stone was strewn in dusty shards across the floor.

The great workshop lay beyond, filled with infernal light. No sooner than the door was broken than ungodly smoke, smelling like the discharge of failed alchemy, vomited from the entranceway and began to fill up the corridor like a grey, gloaming serpent.

Cali stepped into the smog, and into the dwelling place of the Fires of Manifestation.

Her heart hammered in her chest as she approached the gleaming fire that lay through the veils of smoke. The room was as she remembered it, a place of elemental force, at war and yet in harmony, for it was the very chaos of these unions that brought new creation. Though her body was stronger by far than when she had last come to this place, sweat still sheened her flesh, and the heat cut through to the core of her being. The Claw felt as though it were on the brink of melting, the superheated metal talons bubbling slightly, as though their magics might be undone, reduced to glowing slag. Stabs of pain travelled up her arm.

The Claw is afraid, Cali realised. *This is the one place it can be undone . . .*

At the nameless plinth, where no mark, letter, language, or symbol corrupted the essential purity, she paused. The faggots stolen from the nameless tree residing in Pe'kar's court—*no, in Cali's Diadem,* my *palace!*—glowed with everlasting heat; they had been lit since before memory. Perhaps they might burn until long after memory ceased.

Cali . . .

It was The Claw, pleading with her. She had originally come to the palace to destroy the talisman, after all. The weapon had been a danger to her. All it took was one madman to pay its price, and they would be capable of standing against her. But now *she* wore The Claw.

But you should destroy it now, she thought. *If you don't, its madness will take hold. You have used it to defeat the last true threat in Carcosa. You don't need it any more.* True, she would mourn the loss of her arm, but there were many artificers in the Six-Ringed City who could fashion her a new limb, one that did not require her to sell her soul.

Cali, don't. I am your strength. You need me.

She raised The Claw, hovering it over the Fires. The Fires had the power to create that which should not exist, but they also had the power to destroy, to unmake what had been made, to return things to their base elements. Such was the quixotic and bidirectional process of creativity, for only by breaking things down could new forms come into existence.

Cali, you make a grave mistake. You need me.

"I don't need you," Cali snarled. "I have won. No one can stop me now. Even if my sister survived Golgon, she was never a match for me, even before I inherited Pe'kar's power. You have served your purpose."

She was about to plunge her hand—or rather, The Claw—into the heart of the Fires, to suffer the mind-bending agony of its removal, when it spoke one last time, uttering only two words.

The only two words that could have halted her.

Alan Chambers.

She raised The Claw, gritting her teeth, enraged that it knew already how to play upon her mind.

"He is dead," she said. Had she not said the same thing to Hao? And to Liliya? Why did everyone insist Alan was not dead? Terrible doubt gnawed at her heart like an insidious parasite, fattening itself in the vessels of her aorta, a blood-drinker just like she was, feeding on the life of others. *You must master doubt! These are all falsities, tricks, lies, illusions. He cannot be alive!*

But he is, The Claw said. *I was connected to him. I bonded with him at the level of spirit. He is alive. And he is coming.*

"How?"

I do not know. But you will not be able to stand against him without me. I know him. I know his weaknesses.

A howl of frustration left her throat. How could this be possible? Yet with every second that passed, she knew it to be true, she knew it was not only possible, but inevitable.

"How can I defeat him? If he can come back from death, how can I destroy him?"

She sensed The Claw's dark pleasure then, a malice fermented over eons, ripening into a poison so deadly that reality itself might be drugged with a single drop, bent out of shape, like a mind in the throes of hallucinogens, ripped from the moorings of sanity and plunged into a carnival world of horrors.

It is his spirit that survives, The Claw answered. *So, it is his spirit we must kill.*

Cali smiled, her face lit from below by the flames of all creation and un-creation.

"We destroy his spirit and we destroy him?"

Yes.

"But how might we destroy the spirit?"

It is simple: bring me to him. There is no substance I may not rend. Flesh, stone, spirit, mind, dreams, all are nothing before my power. I am The Claw that grasps reality. Nothing can escape my reach. Direct your intent beyond flesh to the soul, and I shall do the rest. Whatever form he comes in, I shall be waiting.

"Do this," Cali said. "And I shall obey you. I shall set you free." She cared for nothing else now, only the surety that Alan was dead.

The Claw trembled.

Even unto the end of all things? Even unto the dying of the last star?

"Yes," Cali whispered, a near-sexual heat kindling in the sacrum of her spine. "Even unto that darkest of ends."

The Claw ignited as Cali gave a cry like deepest satiation, lightning sheathing its talons, blazing brighter even than the Fires of its making, which seemed now but a guttering candle, flickering feebly in the winds of armageddon.

CHAPTER 18
FROM THE RUBBLE

THE DUST HAD not yet settled. She was half-blind, blood running from her wounded eyelids down her face, dust choking her lungs like a deathly pox, but Cassilda cared naught. She had lost her father, lost Alan Chambers. She could not lose Petruccio as well.

She pulled free from LeBarron and ran to the mountainous pile of rubble now shattering multiple streets. She began digging with her bare hands, making the grunting, sobbing sounds of a distraught animal. The mummer hesitated a moment, then joined her. He seemed to know that it was futile to try and stop her. And besides, all was lost—they had nothing better to be doing than gaze on the face of their friend one last time.

Like a feral creature, she dug. Her fingers were soon bloodied. But the pain there was nothing against the pain burning in her heart. Since Alan had died, Petruccio had been her rock, seeming to represent the very foundations of Carcosa itself. So long as he endured, there was hope. But now, the tower had fallen upon him, with all the catastrophic omen that entailed.

"You can't go. Not to the underworld. Not yet. You promised we would face Cali. Truly face her." She screamed in primal rage. How dare Cali deny Petruccio a real death, treat them as mere bugs to be crushed. Cassilda had seen the scorn in her sister's face, as though she resented even the paltry effort it cost her to shatter their world.

Cassilda's grief proved incendiary fuel for the inferno of her soul. Anger incinerated the ugly remains of sorrow and despair. Anger made her into a shining glyph, one LeBarron had to withdraw from, afraid to touch or look upon. With her bare hands she shattered stone, digging and digging. Though her magic had been used up, she still had within her the magic of the spirit, with all its ebbs and tides, a vast and illimitable ocean that was more fire than liquid.

"Your duty is not done, Petruccio. You once served my sister, but now you shall serve me. Come on!"

The minutes of her toil felt like hours, but she cared not. Her fingers were stripped almost to the bone. LeBarron dug elsewhere, unable to come near her for how her flesh shone. She could not get the image of dungbeetles upon a shitheap out of her head. Cali had reduced them to this. Scrabbling in the wreckage for the meagre glint of hope. She screamed again and put all her strength into the dig. Deeper down, the stones were larger, harder to move. Without magic, she was physically frailer. Her tiny arms could barely hoist the huge boulders out from their moorings. But she let nothing deter her.

Then, like a miner striking a gold vein, she saw that glinting hope.

Beneath the layers of grey, lifeless rock—for indeed, the soul of Golgon had been destroyed as it was toppled, leaving what had once been an organic, living thing as mere dust and materials—she glimpsed the twinkle of pure diamond.

"Yes!"

She redoubled her efforts, resembling a demented rabbit in the throes of making their protective burrow. LeBarron saw her frenzy and approached, albeit gingerly, now helping her with the heavier stones.

"Yes, yes, yes, yes!" She was manic, crazed even. But she would not stop. Blood slicked her arms to the elbow and covered her battle-dress.

One by one, she removed the stones, revealing more of Petruccio, who lay like a shell buried beneath sand, an immaculate, glimmering jewel sunken in a coarse ocean. The armour had held strong. Nowhere was it dented. Not for the first time, she wondered how the suit had been made, how diamond had been smelted in such a way that it could be formed like liquid metal into plates and ergonomic fittings. Magic, of course, but of what kind she did not know. And who was the author? A mystery that only the city itself could know. And the city was soon to be dead, unable to speak its secrets.

She brushed the dust from Petruccio's face. He was smeared in blood, his granitic features blank and ashen.

"I'll help you," LeBarron said.

Together, they attempted to drag Petruccio from the mooring of stone. But the effort proved vain. For one thing, the dwarf seemed heavier than the planet itself, a crippling weight, as though his muscles were fashioned from solid marble. In addition, his legs and one hand were caught, trapped in crushing vices of stone. Cassilda and LeBarron renewed their digging, carefully removing the blocks and bricks from around his limbs. A starchild, Petruccio glowed at the heart of his stone womb. Again they tried to move him, but something was still stuck: a piece of the vambrace caught on a lip of jagged rock.

"Come on!" Cassilda shrieked.

They pulled and pulled. Petruccio slid free. Then came the effort of actually lifting him. Both LeBarron and Cassilda uttered piteous groans, the actor's veins nearly bursting with the strain, but eventually they delivered Petruccio's corpse, a cosmic birth, the city giving up the promised child with its last breath of life.

Cassilda held him in her bloody arms. LeBarron stood over her shoulder, his face a mask that had no parallel in any mummer's show. She thought they must resemble a family: she the mother, LeBarron the father, and Petruccio so small that he seemed a child. *Our dead child. The death of all hope.*

Cassilda's wails shook the city as resoundingly as Cali's harp. She could not hold them back. Her lament was a song without melody, without resolution, without meaning except to express the inexpressible. In mourning Petruccio, she mourned Alan truly, mourned her father, mourned Roland, mourned all who had been lost along the way. A shudder seemed to pass through Carcosa, the tattered banners to cease their flying as the great winds paid a tribute of silence to the one who had given all to defend the city.

And then Petruccio took a breath.

Cassilda could have screamed, such was the shock that ran through her. Her soul left her body and hovered behind, observing all as one might a dream. LeBarron turned so white it seemed he had become a page, bled of ink, returned to wordless infancy.

Petruccio's eyes opened and he turned his face slowly to her, blinking away dust and blood and grit. Then the smallest smile spread across his face, like a chink in solid stone, a crack so small

117

most would miss it entirely. Cassilda wept anew, for nothing that could wring tears from a weary soul quite like the return of something they loved.

"Petruccio," she whispered. "You came back."

"I was never gone," he said. "The city saved me. For what purpose, I do not know. Perhaps to face Cali one last time."

Cassilda nodded. Tears still ran down her face, but she was nodding, fire burning in her crimson-flecked eyes.

"She has taken the palace," LeBarron said.

"Then let us face her there," Cassilda said. "Let us call her out onto the steps and challenge her. I'm tired of running. Tired of chasing. Tired of all of it!"

Petruccio nodded.

"I will be with you."

"And me," LeBarron added, quietly.

Cassilda helped Petruccio to stand.

"For Carcosa," she said.

Petruccio smiled again, sadder than she had ever seen him.

"For your father."

Together, they made their way towards the palace, and the final doom that awaited.

They found their way to the foot of the palace soon enough. They met Calian soldiers on the way, but most were too distracted with their grisly work to pose any obstacle. Cassilda, LeBarron, and Petruccio left them to their desecrations. The Trio cared only about Cali, and about meeting whatever end God intended for them.

Cassilda wanted to call out to her sister, but she found instead Cali was already waiting for them, emerging from the dark doorway at the top of the steps like a stygian goddess from the first void.

Cassilda had never known hatred like she felt now, had never boiled with such insane anger. It was all she could do not to run at her sister like a wild animal, to try to bite and scratch her to death, but such an attack would be useless. They had come this far, been granted one more opportunity, they could not waste it. *LeBarron need only strike her once,* Cassilda thought. *His blade could end this . . .* She knew that it was likely she and Petruccio would die in the process of distracting her long enough for the actor to stab Cali, to that land a single blow, but it would be worth it for such an end to be accomplished.

Thunder rumbled in the sky. Lightning forked. It seemed to Cassilda that the elements were enjoying the spectacle of Cali's triumph, lending theatre to her victory. Or perhaps her sister had grown so powerful that the weather itself bent to her will, inspired by her malice to hurl all its abuse down upon the forsaken citadel.

Cali looked down on them, and there was no pity in her eyes, nor even surprise. Her flesh seemed cloaked in a black radiance, like a shimmering armour of the spirit.

"I grow weary of these encounters, sister," Cali said, and her voice nearly caused Cassilda to flinch, for it harmonised with the thunder, crackled with a current not of electricity but raw magic. The Claw upon Cali's arm was so bright it was painful to look upon, an enigma clothed in the magmatic white of heaven's splendour. Seeming to draw thunderbolts, lightning zagged out of the sky dangerously close to her, but never quite hitting. *Her sister could likely catch a bolt if it struck true,* Cassilda thought. *She has become invincible.* But she did not envy Cali. Even now, she partly pitied her. What had she given to unlock such powers? *Everything and more.*

"Then let us end it," Cassilda said, more bravely than she felt. "It was always war between us. Now we finish the fight."

Cali did not smile. Gone were all her pretensions and grandiloquences, it seemed. What was left was a cold power so potent the air hissed, the stone trembled, and the sky screamed at her mere presence.

"You imagine there will be some heroic charge, a worthy sacrifice, a contest between us," Cali said. "But there will be no such thing." She raised The Claw, and Cassilda heard a humming sound, as though the personification of power drew in breath before expelling a gale that would strip flesh from its bones. The analogy was not far from the truth. The Claw's glow grew even more eye-searing, but Cassilda refused to avert her eyes; she would look death in the face, even if it burned her eyes out of the sockets. "Your deaths shall be ignominious," Cali said. "As The Claw wills, so mote it be."

Cali made a gesture with The Claw like swatting away a fly. A beam of light shot out so fast toward them that she did not even manage to blink before it was imminent. LeBarron and Petruccio were also caught by its speed, dumbfoundedly moving to evade with the pace of slugs—vain and useless. Cassilda could have screamed had she time. The beam would strike; all three of them would die instantly.

A great white shield came between them and death. Suddenly it appeared, forming out of the air with all the ceremony of a magician plucking a playing card from nowhere.

With a gong-like sound, the Claw's beam ricocheted off the shield and rebounded into the heavens, losing none of its force. Lightning and cloud itself were scoured by the passage of The Claw's dreadful light, a black hole opening like a bullet-wound in the sky.

And then something emerged from that wound, spiralling down. At first, it seemed a turgid blackness, like a thousand dark serpents all coiling about one another, a spillage of worms tossed from some celestial chariot. But then the serpents began to unite, to mingle, forming a dense black cloud that held a gleaming pearl at its heart, a white visage harbouring two ruby gems for eyes.

Cassilda's breath caught in her throat. Her muscles spasmed. Her legs nearly gave way beneath the weight of revelation. *How? How could he be here?*

But her awe was not the equal of LeBarron's, whose eyes went wide with terrified wonder, whose flesh seemed to revolt against itself, to wish to flee the moorings of his skeleton and dance under the raincloud descending toward them like a living storm.

Thunder illuminated the god's passage, like paving stones of electricity. The mask that shone at the heart of the mien was brighter even than Petruccio's diamond armour, its expression morphing into a jester's glee as it came upon the city like a hurricane: furious, colossal, draconian, the black hand of god.

The new arrival spiralled towards the earth, towards where Cali stood nearly dumbstruck, gazing up at the cacophony of shadow.

LeBarron let out a cry of jubilation and despair, a cry in which all the dark paradoxes of the universe were resolved, utterly unmaking his mind in a moment of unequalled sublimity.

"The Stranger!" he cried. "The Stranger has come!"

CHAPTER 19
THE FLOWER OF CARCOSA

THE JOY OF the garden had ended; he had departed Eden. The only solace was the thought that one day he might return and take his place upon the forever-blooming tree, one with the Great Serpent, and one with the souls of the great men and women who had gone before him. But that was another tale, to be told another time. He had to be somewhere else.

But he could not seem to find the way.

The darkness across which he travelled—in a form of flight that felt less like flying and more like swimming through layers of sable cloth—was more impenetrable even than the icy forgetfulness of Lake Hali's waters. There, his consciousness had been obliterated. But here, it was alive, so alive that the canvas of nothingness became maddening. His mind searched and probed ceaselessly for some break in the monotonous emptiness, but he found no exit, no feature, no texture, no sound, only an endless landscape as barren as death itself.

I must go back, he thought. *I must find a way.*

But there was no path to be followed, no golden thread of light. God had lifted him up into the darkness of existence once more, and he was again a spirit germinating in the womb of creation, but without a physical body to be born into. *Is this my fate? To wander the darkness forever?*

No. He had to believe there was a way out, however slim, however narrow, however implausible to find.

Time stretched and contracted simultaneously. He drifted upon eddies of darkness, inchoate yet palpable, oceanic tides in the Great Nothing. He plumbed to unfathomable depths only to find himself soaring. He flew into the upper reaches only to arrive at a murky basement, a gutter-flow of cosmic sewage dragged down into a whirlpool mouth. He would not go to that place. It filled him with dread. But at least he had found a break in the monotony.

His mind wandered as his spirit did. He thought of everything that had brought him to this point. He remembered every lifetime, every fallacy, every failure, every regret. He remembered his triumphs too, few though they were. Passing the trials set by Cali. Gaining entry to Carcosa. Taking The Claw and using it to save those he called his friends.

A kiss with Cassilda under a black star.

It was the memory of that kiss that broke through the darkness. All at once, he arrived at a blooming strangeness in the midst of primordial emptiness, a lone flower breaking through the stone of a long-abandoned cathedral. If he'd had breath, it might have caught in his throat. If he'd eyes, they might have widened. Hair might have stood on end, had he possessed limbs or flesh. As it was, his spirit convulsed with something near to orgasm, but purer, the sensation evoked by the imminence of beauty.

A flower bloomed in this cosmic sewage. From the filth of black nothingness there rose a white blossom. It resembled no flower Abracadabra knew of. Its petals were seventeen in number. Gold spots, like beauty marks, adorned its delicate flesh. Its blushing stigmas blew in a wind that had no name nor origin. The beauty of it ravished him, arrested his constant flight, making him a pillar of stillness in the midst of ancient chaos.

He knew, without explanation, that the flower was his beloved Cassilda. In the garden, he had shed his attachments, shed his sense of ego and self, shed his fear of death, yet it was as if the universe—that great Serpent God—now returned to him the one attachment he needed, the one that was forgivable in the eyes of transcendent divinity: love.

I love Cassilda! No spiritual journey, no divine revelation, could unmake that reality. Indeed, the purpose of his spiritual journey had merely been to arrive again at this knowledge, to purify his love so that it could bloom even in the stultifying void.

Had he a face, tears would have scalded it.

But the flower was dying. Under the cosmic pressures of this purgatorial interstice, the petals were wilting, shrivelling, declining. Where at first the flower had stood tall and proud as any tree—a magnificent white-crowned blossom—now it resembled a white-haired beggar, hunched over and beaten down by the vicissitudes of life. Petals fell from its corona. The stigma drooped like the lolling tongue of a disease-ridden dog.

I have to save it, he thought. *I have to save her.*

And in that urgency, a pathway was revealed, for in the drooping flowerhead he beheld a doorway. As once he had descended through the head of a xanthimum into the secret city of Alar, now he was being called back via a similar pathway into the secret illusion of existence.

Cassilda! I am coming! Cassilda!

He was moving again, no longer transfixed by the flower's beauty. He was flying toward it, hurtling at a meteoric speed. The flower opened its mouth to receive him, and swifter than thought itself he was swallowed by a cosmic throat. As the darkness began to brighten, acidic reality flushing upward to meet him, a thought-memory from a former life emerged from the recesses of his brain: that the God Shiva held the universe in his throat.

But he could not swallow because it was poison.

Geometries drawn upon the black canvas of space. Cloud, water, earth, all were one. Midnight blue, purple, black, all the most beautiful colours, ribboning, folding, undulating, lapping like waves, rising like smoke from a flame, burning and fizzling, inchoate yet coagulate, thicker than honey, lighter than air, deeper than water. The universe eternally transmuting into something else. Consciousness the only fixed point. The "I", but no "I" of ego, of Self, of identity, a formless "I" that was also an "eye", that watched, that sensed, but cast no judgement or aspersion. *Is this death?* The thought rising from the darkness—no fear attached, no worrying. Simply a question, and the resounding answer: *YES!* A strange joy to it, the colours strobing, and sounds travelling through the deep like great barges composed of music, hummings and tinklings, cascades, bass notes—singing. The "I" felt like singing too, though there was no throat with which to sing, pure consciousness only, adrift in the miasmal yet beautiful sea of many colours.

THE KING OF CARCOSA

And then it ended.

Or rather, it began anew. Abracadabra found himself in a garden. But it was not the Eden he had left behind in some far-distant galaxy. This was another garden, a place of tragedy and woe: The Garden of Grim Knowledge.

The disberry tree that had once bloomed here—a favourite of The King In Yellow—still lay shrivelled and dead. Its branches looked like blackened bones burned in a cremation ritual. In fact, many of the garden's flowers were dying, whether because the poison of Cali's arrow was spreading to the rest of the flora through the tree's infected roots, or whether through lack of maintenance. The dimetrodon who had once happily haunted this secret corner of the palace lay dead and gutted, flies buzzing about his slack-jawed face.

Abracadabra had no time to mourn the garden, however. He knew the moment of action was imminent. He had to find Cassilda, find his friends, and stop Cali before it was too late.

The sounds of conflict shook the palace stone. He saw the sky was a catastrophe of light, ruin, and storm. The wind bore screams to his ear, the dire song of night-worshipping demons. The hour was late. He had almost tarried too long in the realm of the dead.

He made his way through a door into the palace proper. The hallways were bloody confusion. The bodies of courtiers and soldiers lay strewn about. Some were hacked to pieces. Some seemed to have died from pure terror. *Cali,* Abracadabra thought. *It must be her.*

He stooped to examine one of the corpses. The wound-marks were strange. Five horizontal slices had opened up their belly, spilling intestinal worms across the ancient stone. His heart drummed a beat of thunder. He could not believe what he was seeing, *didn't want* to believe, but there was only one possibility.

The Claw!

So Cali had taken the cursed artefact from him and now wielded it herself. Truly she was lost if she'd resorted to such dire means. He remembered all too well the dark temptations of The Claw, and he knew with sadness that for all her many gifts, Cali was not the equal of resisting them.

Abracadabra hastened through the palace, its geography returning to him in hazy fragments. The carnage was harrowing, even to one who had been to the edge of the universe and back, who had fought in several chthonian wars, who had borne the burden of The Claw.

He found a living courtier. They were using a wall to support them as they fled, though where one could go, considering the scale of destruction, Abracadabra did not know. Perhaps they were looking for a friend among the piles of dismembered corpses? Perhaps they were looking for Cassilda, like he was, a beacon in the darkness. The courtier wore flowing purple robes, though one side was stained red. A bloody wound in their torso leaked gore Their face was a mask of pain that mounted with each shuffling step.

"Can I help you?" Abracadabra said.

The courtier did not reply.

Thunder shook the palace. Abracadabra heard a song rise, though it was more like a dirge, the guttural throat-music of Tibetan monks, spelling the sound of creation. Magic!

"Tell me, is the battle already lost? Where is the exit?" Abracadabra said. *And where is Cali?*

Still the courtier ignored him.

He might be deaf, Abracadabra thought. With such potent magics being thrown around, it was no wonder. He had thought himself deaf for a moment when he had first heard Cali play her magical instrument, transporting him to Carcosa's walls.

Abracadabra walked up to the courtier and placed a hand on his shoulder. He knew there was a risk that this might startle the courtier, but he wanted to help him, and he needed help himself. But his desire to help was soon executed by the guillotine blade of realisation.

His hand, which he had thought to be substantial and enfleshed, passed *through* the courtier.

The courtier continued to hobble onward, clutching his wound, oblivious. Abracadabra recoiled.

No. No, no, no.

He looked down at his hands and saw . . . nothing. He was invisible.

"Hello?" he said, desperation making his voice a tear in reality. "Hello!" He bellowed with all his power, but the courtier did not respond.

THE KING OF CARCOSA

Invisible, without physical body, and mute. God had sent him back as a mere spirit, a ghost. He fell to his knees—though in truth there was nothing to fall to. He was a mere disembodied entity. Being, consciousness, but nothing more. The cruelty of it almost made him mad. Had he a head, he would have dashed it on the stone walls and ended his life once and for all.

No, it cannot end this way. It cannot be.

But the more he thought on it, the more it made sense. His body had been cast into the Place of Forever Falling, after all. There was no recovery from that place. And he could not fashion a new body out of nothing. Only his spirit had endured Cali's deathblow. So, only his spirit came back.

How long he wept there, he did not know. He listened to the sound of his city dying, the screams and torment so apocalyptic that soon it became parodic; he could have laughed, laughed like a crazed lunatic in an insane asylum—equally ignored by the world.

But even now, there was hope. A small hand touched his shoulder, the very same way he had hoped to touch the courtier. He turned and saw a girl, no older than ten, staring down at him with compassionate eyes. He barely had time to register the strange wonder of her loving face when he saw others, all gathering behind her, all looking directly at him. They were translucent, a grey-shimmer to their flesh—though it was not flesh in truth. They were naked, one and all, and yet their nakedness seemed not a crudity but an innocence. A familiar tingle ran through him, under his skin, for though he had no skin he *felt* like he did; the sensation was like an electrical current finding its way to his arteries, carried along the tributaries of a body he no longer possessed. He'd felt this once before. Then it clicked.

The shades! The ghosts looking down on him were the invisible shades of the city, and he was one of them.

Slowly, he stood. He ruffled the little girl's hair, and she smiled. The shades opened their arms and embraced him. He felt warmth—though dull, though faint—and an overwhelming joy bloomed in his heart like the darkest and most secret of saplings, planted in the dead of night beneath a black moon. Now he understood one of the final riddles of the city. The circle was complete, and he had passed through all five levels: from coprophage to outcast to courtier to cannibal and at last to shade.

Even as they held one another, these invisible and unseen

hands of Carcosa, more were gathering, coming through the walls, collecting like filaments to a magnet, hundreds, thousands, tens of thousands, perhaps even more. Abracadabra felt he was the lightning rod for an energy so massive it was overwhelming. Still more shades came, of every age, shape, colour, gender, cast, and character.

Eventually, they released him from their embrace, standing in a circle.

"What must I do?" he asked.

None of them made reply with words. Instead, one of their number, a stern looking man, raised his hand and pointed with a single finger. Abracadabra turned, and saw a corridor stretching in the direction his finger indicated.

Walk then. Walk to meet my final fate.

Abracadabra set off.

And the shades of Carcosa followed him.

CHAPTER 20
BREAKING THE MASK

CALI LOOKED TO the skies and saw The Stranger, Mazael, descending on her with all the bluster a false god could muster.

"The Pallid Mask was broken," Cali remarked.

"I wear no mask!" The Stranger screamed.

So you wish to riddle prettily with me? she thought.

The Stranger had evidently found a way to reforge his artefact, but such arcane talismans would matter little against her might.

She raised The Claw.

"Begone!"

The blast that left The Claw wounded the sky forever. The black cloud that had so ominously filled the heavens from horizon to horizon burst into flames, a meteoric incandescence that illuminated the city like a maddened sun knocked from its fixed place. But the meteor was burning away, shrivelling, disintegrating as it fell, the great mass shrinking and shrinking until only a glimmering pearl remained, a shining mask with nothing behind it. The mask alone clattered to the steps of the palace, skidding to Cali's feet. She smiled darkly. Then she raised her foot and stamped upon it, shattering the Pallid Mask as though it had been made of nothing more durable than fine china.

LeBarron collapsed. His mighty sword fell to the ground, ineffectual as a toothpick. He spasmed and foamed, in the throes of a seizure. It was no surprise to Cali. He had worshipped The Stranger as his true god, and worshippers could not survive the death of their idols, however false.

Cali shifted her gaze to her sister, who met Cali's imperious stare with admirable courage. *So you will die a worthy death then. Quick, humiliatingly so, but worthy.*

By Cassilda's side, Petruccio stared with equal defiance.

"Petruccio, you were my faithful servant once," Cali said. "Be my faithful servant again. You have shown me you have such potential . . . There's no need for you to die here."

The dwarf spat on the ground.

Cali smiled.

"Very well." Her eyes returned coldly to Cassilda.

"No offer I make will persuade you from insanity, sister."

Cassilda showed teeth. She knelt and put a hand on LeBarron, who still twitched and drooled upon the floor. Though his convulsions stilled somewhat, it seemed Cassilda's magical powers could not prevent his seizure. Perhaps because it was an ailment not of the body but of a broken mind and spirit. Perhaps because she had no magic left.

Cassilda straightened. She and Petruccio shared a look, a single nod. Cali knew that they had resigned themselves to the foolish dream of a noble death. So be it. Cali would not mock them as she had before; she would give them what they sought. She would not kill them from afar or trample them underfoot. She would be a generous god and slay them with her own divine hand. She would sheath The Claw in their blood and then drink whatever remained.

Petruccio drew up *Hope Reborn* from the ground. The sword was near twice his height, but he wielded it like he was born to it. Cassilda sheathed her fists in ebullient light. Calian soldiers moved to intercept them, but Cali barked a command, and the army halted, as obedient as though they were marionettes, and she the puppetmaster guiding their strings.

Cassilda gritted her teeth, hatred written on her face as clearly as death was written in Cali's eyes.

"You may think you've won, Cali," Cassilda said, with quiet fury. "But when you kill me now, you'll only prove Father right. And that will be your everlasting defeat."

Cassilda screamed and ran up the steps toward Cali, fists glowing with magic; Petruccio followed suit, raising his stolen sword.

Cali answered their charge with a single word that detonated with the force of a split atom.

"*Kneel!*"

THE KING OF CARCOSA

The potency of her aura flashed out from her body, a dazzling light, but also a blanket of lead, inescapable gravity, flattening all to the ground.

The thousands congregated at the foot of the palace, like eager tourists to witness some carnival performance, were all forced prostrate, worms beneath the gaze of the divine Beast that was Cali, Black Empress, Vampire Goddess, and wielder of The Cursed Claw.

CHAPTER 21
THE ORDEAL OF THE ABYSS

L EBARRON LAY LOWEST of all, a worm not only in mind but in shape, a drooling thing quivering upon the stone. *God is dead. God is dead. God is dead. God is dead.*

His heart was a wormhole, his reality shattered like a grave-urn . . .

Petruccio tried to rise but could not. Not even his prodigious strength was a match for the enchantment of Cali's aura. This was it, then: the end.

A strange peace found him. All his life he'd believed himself a failure, a small speck of dust in the macrocosm of reality, inconsequential, worthy only of servitude. But now, facing death, he realised how much he had accomplished, how much earned. He had become a powerful magician. He had helped Alan Chambers obtain The Claw. He had found the pigment and passed its trials. He had won wars. Been recognised by the King In Yellow Himself. He had ventured into the heart of the lands of Blue Light, to the very throne of the Demon King himself, and he had won respect from the lieutenants of Pe'kar. And he had stood before Cali without fear and rivalled a god—if only for a moment. To die now was no shame. He had given all and proved more than almost any man living. Whatever suffering awaited, he would accept it as an accolade, the same way one wore their scars with pride . . .

THE KING OF CARCOSA

Cassilda found a different sort of acceptance to Petruccio. Whereas he accepted his fate with the grace of one who had lived a magnificent life, she accepted hers with the bleakness of one who had given up all hope. Her thoughts revolved around her wedding night, the rape that had taken place. She had been subject to violation all her life, it seemed; this was no different. It was pointless to fight against it. Pointless to try. Life was a great, filthy hand that desecrated all souls cursed with the sin of existence. The Claw—what better metaphor could there be for the disgusting nature of reality? A thing that groped, choked, scratched, maimed, and crushed. *Let this be my last torture, my last torment. Let this final rape take all from me and leave me in the bliss of nothingness.*

But one rising thought broke through the pall.

I'm sorry, Alan. I'm sorry!

CHAPTER 22
EGO-DEATH

H E WALKED WITH the countless spirits, the silent phantoms of the city, behind him. The shades led Abracadabra to the palace entrance. When he emerged from it, he almost fell down again, could have wept for a thousand years.

The walls of the city had been brought low. The spires had been toppled and cracked. A thousand times a thousand souls knelt before the palace steps, bowing before a figure so terrible his spirit could barely tolerate comprehension of them.

As much as he hated her, Alan could not deny Cali's splendour. He beheld a goddess incarnate, an empress of darkest midnight, like Babylon glimpsed in the vision of St. John, yet greater, a star outshining the visions of all earthly prophets, with a void at her heart that could swallow all other lights. Her right hand was no hand but a glowing talisman, a cruel artefact that looked like a spider sculpted from the blackest starfire.

The last of the Carcosan defenders had been rounded up like cattle. And now Cassilda, Petruccio, LeBarron, and the few remaining soldiers were hemmed in by the Calians at the foot of the palace. Calian and Carcosan alike knelt, bent beneath the weight of an invisible mantle, one Abracadabra knew was called "aura".

"Now is the moment arrived!" Cali cried. "Now is the moment I have so long awaited! The black planet is mine! Bow before thy new goddess! Those who kiss my feet shall be raised up! And those who do not shall be cast into the endless void!"

Abracadabra threw himself at Cali, clawed at her, tried to grip her upraised hand to prevent her lowering it, but all was useless. He could no more move her than a child's breath move a mountain.

133

THE KING OF CARCOSA

He fled down the steps, followed by the shades. He saw LeBarron, eyes rolled into the back of his head, deranged and lost. Petruccio, his face a solemn mask of one who did not fear death. And Cassilda, his dearest love, lost in black despair. He collapsed before her, a penitent before an altar found unexpectedly in a foreign land. She was as beautiful as he remembered, as willowy, as delicate, as gracious, even spattered in blood and filth. But what broke his heart was how her eyes shone vacantly as a pit's slimed walls, how her face carried nothing of the life and power he had fallen in love with. Despair lived there now, having exiled joy and hope forever. She was a shell, and *he* had made her this way.

"Cassilda!" he whispered. "Please hear me! Cassilda! Please!"

She made no reply.

He sobbed.

"Cassilda, please! You have to get up! You have to do something!" He tried to grip her hands, tried to touch her face, tried to wipe away the tears that now streamed from her lifeless eyes. But he was a ghost, nothing more.

He went to Petruccio, and tried to call upon the dwarf, but there was no response.

"As my will—!" Cali began, then hesitated, perhaps to savour the moment, perhaps because the sheer rush of power flooding through her was too much to wield.

Abracadabra turned. Cali stood at the top of the palace steppe, the skies themselves seeming to gravitate towards her, resembling water swirling down a plughole; she was the vacuum that gathered all things to her with the inexorable attraction of pure emptiness.

Abracadabra had to do something, had to stop her. If Cali finished those words, then it would all be over. He knew not the name of her spell, but he could tell its character. She would dominate all in a way that Pe'kar could only have dreamed of.

I must do something.

But as a shade there was nothing he could do.

Abracadabra screamed. Was this his fate? To have been brought back, to have returned from death, only to powerlessly witness the fall of his world, the death of the woman he loved. Was this the terrible laughter of the King In Yellow, the doom-song of the forbidden-named god, the curse of his father? He had conquered death only to know the blackest despair.

He screamed from the depths of his soul. And none heard him.

Save for one.

Amidst the deaf throng, kneeling, subjugated, and prostrate before the shining potentate—who even now raised her enchanted hand to deliver the *coup de grace*, a sign that would rewrite not only the destiny of Carcosa but also its past—amidst those blind to the secret truth of all universes, helpless, cowed, and broken by the Black Goddess, there was one who heard Abracadabra's cry.

And his name was LeBarron.

Some thread still tethered the two men—perhaps not only blood, but a bond of secret shared identity, a knowledge of the dark performance of life, that one's face was merely a mask, and what lay behind the face: another mask still. This and only this was the salvation of all, the one thin, thin hope to which Abracadabra now clung with all his will.

"A-Alan?" LeBarron whispered.

"LeBarron!" Abracadabra cried, joy singing in his heart. "LeBarron it's me. I'm here!"

LeBarron smiled, his drool-flecked face only making him look more insane.

"I knew . . . somehow, I always knew it would come to this," LeBarron whispered.

"What do you mean?"

LeBarron licked his lips.

"When I died, I left pieces of me behind. But now I know why . . . I was making room for you, Alan. I was making room for you."

Abracadabra's being trembled.

"You mean . . . ?"

"You must come into me, Alan. Come into me. I am a mummer. I am a body with no soul, I must be formless to take on whatever shape is demanded of me. You are a soul with no body. You shall wear me. And through me, you shall deliver the city, as has always been foretold."

The actor's eyes searched for Abracadabra, but it seemed though he could hear the spirit, he could not see him. The deepest sorrow Abracadabra had ever witnessed lived in LeBarron's strangely haunting features, but it was a resolved sorrow, a sorrow of determination, like hard-shelled life stirring beneath the crushing pressure of the waves.

"But . . ."

"There's no time left, Alan. The moment is almost arrived.

Possess me. You know how. Come into me." LeBarron's voice rose with every word. The sorrow in his eyes was transforming into a kind of inner light.

"It will be my greatest performance, Alan. The crowning achievement of my career. My final bow upon the stage . . . to be both player and played, both face and mask. O, what a delight it shall be!"

"You would make the ultimate sacrifice?"

"Yes," LeBarron whispered. *"For the way of sacrifice makes man whole."*

And in that instance, they became One.

CHAPTER 23
THE POINT OF POWER

"A S MY WILL—" she uttered, then had to stop, for the power that surged through her was almost too much to bear. Magic coursed through her blood, as though she were the beating heart of the cosmos, the source and end-point of all tributaries, the completion of the great ouroboros itself.

Cali raised her hand—The Claw itself—the sky roared. When she brought it down, all her enemies would be destroyed; those who remained would be bound to her will, with no more agency than the undead servants Cassilda had once wielded to defend her lost city. This was Cali's final and blackest incantation. This, the sum of all her works. *I am arrived here and now! All is fulfilled! Now! Now! Now!*

But then she heard sound—no, more than a sound: *music.* Doleful, pitiful, yet also terrible and thunderous, as though the god of death had written his own eulogy. From whence it came, she could not determine; the air itself seemed to breathe with the liquid song. Sonorous voices—utterly numberless—were raised in mournful proclamation. Were the stones of the city singing a lament, or did the spirits of the dead cry out to her to stay her hand?

The shades! she thought suddenly. *The shades sing!* But what harm could they do her now? Eerie and eldritch though their music was, echoing out of some deep well of nothingness known only to those without material forms, yet they were powerless to stop her.

She steeled herself: she must bring her hand down, seal the fateful ritual with the final magical gesture, but with thunderous intensity the song of the shades rose, and as if this song were a tide carrying with it a great ship of fools: one soul suddenly stepped forward from the crowd of bowing subjects.

At first, she thought her eyes deceived her. She stood as one dumbstruck, arm still raised. Then she laughed.

"What's this? The failed actor steps forth to defend his city?" She smiled with bloody teeth. "Spare me your theatrics, LeBarron. What little power The Stranger granted you died with him."

LeBarron placed a single foot upon the steps of the palace. Slowly, he raised his eyes to hers. A fury burned there that she had never witnessed before, a rage that was so incandescent it had purified itself, burning away its own chaotic excess and leaving only a spiritual yearning. The light that shone from his face was painful. His beauty was like a scar on reality, a perfection that made all else seem ugliness; she could scarcely stand to look at him.

And that foot upon the first step! How was it possible? How did he resist her aura? No will existed in the world that could counteract the crushing gravity of her power. No, it had to be something else, but what?

"No grand speech?" she said, trying to regain her confidence with mockery. "No drama, no poetry, no monologue?"

LeBarron took another step towards her, ascending the stairs. His face burned like sunlight. The sword in his hand was a fang of the moon's treacherous glow; she knew that weapon, knew who had made it, and feared its terrifying potential.

"Do not test me, LeBarron!" she snapped. "Do not make me wrathful!"

A third step. A fourth. Implacably, he advanced. The audience of Carcosa's millions—and her Calian soldiery—watched in breathless awe, a silence so pronounced it was audible. Yet for Cali there was no silence: the shades continued their dire lamentations, a dirge for the end of things.

"Enough!" she spat. "Go no further!"

But still he defied her, now within a mere ten steps. She had no choice. She must strike him down, or else all would be lost.

She raised The Claw, and a blast of light emitted from her palm. LeBarron swung *Hope Reborn* in an upward arc, the blade intercepting the streak of light, connecting with energy that should not have been solid, and sending the blast careening off into the sky, zig-zagging, drawing new constellations upon the black canvas of the heavens, and finally detonating like the finale of a firework display.

At no point did LeBarron halt in his advance.

Cali shrieked, an ululating battle cry that rose from deep within her. She leapt and brought The Claw slicing down. The universe bent with the motion, as though the gravity of her aura also dragged in air, stone, wood, fire, and metal in its wake.

LeBarron leapt to the side. The Claw struck the ground and a fissure deep as hell's maw split through the palace steps, all the way to the foot, where the obeisant onlookers stared with glittering wonder.

LeBarron was already on the counter-attack. She heard his blade singing through the air. She had no time to dodge, and so she raised The Claw in her right hand. *Hope Reborn* swung from the right-hand side—she stopped it with her palm. The eruption of force from the connection of the two talismans, both forged by Pe'kar with the blackest artistry, caused the remaining edifices of the city to tremble, rent the ground beneath them, widening the fissure, so it seemed they fought over the gulf of Tartarus itself.

Cali leapt back. LeBarron's weapon was longer ranged that hers. She had to be careful.

She raised her fingers and sent a series of small blasts toward him. They writhed through the air like sea serpents cutting through the water. His footing was treacherous. For a moment, she thought he might fall. But then he was somersaulting, leaping so high in the air he seemed more than an acrobat, but a bird, whose feather-light bones enabled him to float on the wind. He was over her head, dropping behind her, his blade already flashing. She intercepted his second attack, this time blocking left with The Claw, and once more the clarion bell of their meeting made Carcosa groan and tremble, made the stars flicker, as though about to fall from their fixed places like mosaic tiles falling the ceiling of a collapsed cathedral. Black lightning shot out from the cruel talons of her machine-hand. But it was answered by purest flame, a white flame that burned so incandescently bright she was forced to recoil, staggering backward, nearly blundering over the edge of the precipitous drops opening in the stairwell.

She expected a reprieve, that LeBarron would fight her cautiously, but she was wrong. His fury seemed to outweigh even hers. He came at her like a white lion, the flame of his sword cutting gashes in her vision. It was all she could do to stay ahead of the weapon. And even though she dodged its strokes, the flame licked at her flesh, sending pain scouring through her overtaxed limbs.

She retreated, working her way back up the steps. She was only defending now, something a weapon like The Claw was not made for. LeBarron's swordsmanship was a dazzle of frenetic cuts and feints, never coming from the same direction twice, never predictable, always reversing and changing, a hypnotic assault as deadly for its beauty as its power and dexterity. *I have to halt the momentum of his attack.*

She caught *Hope Reborn* and gripped it with her talons, arresting the furious back and forth. White flame licked around The Claw's gunmetal fingers. Cali snarled. LeBarron tried to wrench his blade free, but her grip was inexorable. The magical reaction occurring within her palm was an exquisite madness Cali had to turn away from. No sooner did The Claw's dark lightning unfurl then it was quelled by flame, and the two seemed to be mixing, swirling about one another, blending, forming a yin yang of absolute chaos.

She snapped out a kick into LeBarron's face and he fell back, rolling over and over down the steps, stopping inches from a wide rend in the stone. Cali knew she should press the attack, but she was exhausted, so she used the precious seconds of reprieve to gather herself.

"I have to admit, I did not know you could fight like that, LeBarron," she said. "You're wasted on these dreamers. Come to my side." A mocking grin split her face. "You're worthy of being the black goddesses' bride."

LeBarron stood slowly, drawing up his sword. He almost seemed not to see her. His face was a ruin: nose broken, lips split, one eye blackening. Yet, his expression still showed immutable defiance.

Once more he mounted the steps toward her, coming on with the implacability of a thunderstorm. The flickering flame of her fear was now being fanned into an inferno. *What am I so afraid of?* she wondered. She had faced great opponents, faced death a thousand times—even recently at the very gates of the city—but this creeping dread was a special poison, darkly familiar to her. *It's his spirit,* she thought. *I fear his spirit.*

"LeBarron," she said. "LeBarron. Stop. Listen to me. I don't want to kill you."

For once, he *did* stop in his advance, though only for a moment. His eyes met hers, and within them were galaxies.

"You killed my King," LeBarron said. "Great Hastur—*Everlasting His Name!*" He took another step toward her. The flames dancing along his sword seemed to grow ever brighter, whitening to supernova intensity. "Then you killed my friend, Roland."

"Roland died in battle," Cali said. "And my father, whom you call 'King', was an abuser, a *monster!*" Cali hated that she felt tears running down her face. Gods did not weep. Or if they did, it was only to drown cities.

"And Alan?" LeBarron said, with a curiously dark smile.

Cali swallowed.

"I offered him the way of peace a thousand times. He would not take my hand." Her lips curled into a moon-sickle sneer. "You see everything from your own perspective. *You* came to the Six-Ringed City to apprehend me. You could not leave me be."

LeBarron cocked his head.

"If we had left you be, then would you have forgiven Carcosa, taken a place by the side of the Demon King? I think not. I think you were born free, like all men and women, but at some point a hole opened up inside you, and you decided the only way to fill it was by obtaining absolute power."

"How dare you!" Cali spat. "*You,* who want even for a sense of Self! You, who lacks personality, identity, anything that requires courage to uphold!"

His face cracked into a smile.

"I'm not who you think I am."

Cali smirked.

"Is that so? Well, I might say the same to you. You have no idea what my father did to me."

"That may be true, but does one evil turn deserve another?"

"You would wield a child's infant logic against me?"

"Just because it is simple, does not mean it is untrue."

Cali shrieked. She was in motion before the intention to do so became conscious. This time, she drove *him* back. The Claw was a blur of taloned death, streaks of lightning cascading around them as she hacked and slashed with all her fury. LeBarron was forced to retreat, narrowly dodging, intercepting upon occasion with his sword, flame and sparks shooting off and curling into the sky, or else showering the stone steps. Resonances—notes so deep they were almost beyond human hearing—ran through the ground beneath them, lifted into the air. The chorus of the shades was accompanied by the singing of their weapons, a song so terrible its like would never be known again.

LeBarron backed away step after step, crumpling beneath her rage. He tripped as his heel caught the back of a great gash in the stone and he went over backward. The momentum of his fall carried him over the abyss—just barely—and he collapsed on the lower steps. Cali leapt over the fissure and brought The Claw down. LeBarron was not yet beaten, however, for he rolled to one side and then was rising, his blade swinging in an upward vertical cut.

They continued back and forth, sometimes attacking, sometimes on the defensive, their weapons creating a harrowing dirge. The ring of metal on metal, the howl of flame ruptured by lightning, the scream of supernatural elements colliding, formed the symphony of Carcosa's darkest day.

Both fighters were exhausted, sheened in sweat, their eyes wild, manic stars, blistering in the darkness of a universe that was steadily falling apart. The conflict of these two polarities could not go on much longer without reality un-seaming, and indeed, the onlookers below saw those stretched seams, the stitching of existence itself coming undone, revealing guttering oblivions beneath the veil of what was real, fertile as a garden, yet atramentous as the blackest pitch. Locusts spilled out from the scar-tissue of reality. In the white fire were birthed spirits and abominations. These animate dreams and nightmares blindly encoiled the twin warriors, who rushed headlong upon one another with the implacable fury of an ocean upon a cliff-side, yet both were ocean and cliff simultaneously.

And then the deathblow came. LeBarron pushed Cali all the way to the top of the stairs and against one of the pillars, but Cali always fought best when her back was to the wall. Summoning the deepest dregs of her power and courage, she parried his head-splitting swing and drove her foot into LeBarron's knee. The snapping sound could be heard across the citadel, though no scream left LeBarron's lips, as though he were merely a mannequin when all was said and done. The broken leg caused him to stumble, unable to gain proper balance for his next strike.

Cali backhanded with The Claw. Its grisly talons cut flesh with the ease of plucking a flower petal. Blood washed stone. LeBarron staggered back, dropping to one knee and then to his back, his shattered leg jutting at an awkward angle. His stomach had been gashed wide open, entrails spilling like a bleak offering to bloody-handed gods.

"LeBarron," she said, now trying to instil her voice with command, though in truth it wavered. "If you raise your sword to me again, I will show no mercy. I will kill you."

He stared at her, still snarling, defiant, but she could see in his eyes that he knew he was beaten. He had pushed himself to the very limits of his ability, and for that she had admiration, but he was not her equal on the battlefield.

He took a slow, ragged breath.

"Do what thou wilt."

The words struck her like a lightning bolt. The folly of her hubris was laid bare to her in a blinding flash. She realised who lay behind the actor's eyes, who inhabited the body against which she struggled. The prophecy of The Claw had come true. In the storm's strobing radiance, his true face was revealed, a phantom whom she feared more than any living man.

"You!"

"Abracadabra," Alan said.

She raised The Claw, intent on finishing it, but it was too late. He was already lurching up on his broken leg, shattering the joint even more, careless of pain or injury, rising like a serpent to strike.

He drove his sword to the hilt through Cali's stomach.

The goddess's eyes went wide. She opened her mouth, as though to offer some rebuke, and blood welled from her throat in a gory stream. For a moment, she was paralysed, skewered; then, she made a grunting sound, like a frustrated boar attempting to extricate itself from the hunter's spear. She again attempted speech.

"You . . . you think Pe'kar's bile can kill me now? I drank... Pe'kar's blood. His power is mine... I cannot be undone by it."

"Even a snake may be poisoned by its own venom," Alan replied, though he used LeBarron's mouth.

Cali's lips curled in what might have been a smile, a terrible mixture of hatred and admiration.

"You... *bastard* . . . " she said. Her expression softened, almost pleading. "How . . . how did you come back?"

"I met them, Cali. I met all the champions you threw to the wayside. They were there waiting for me. And they helped send me back."

Cali let out a groan, raw pain transmuted into sound. Her face became a mask of contempt that eventually cracked and left something alarmingly like the innocence of a cruel little girl, one who broke her toys and pulled the wings from wasps without knowing the harm she did.

"Please . . . " she said. "Please don't do this."

"I could have loved you," Alan said. "You would have had my loyalty freely, had you not tried to take it by force."

The surprise that awoke upon her face was not unlike the dawn—and a dark pity stabbed Alan to the core of his spiritual being.

He leaned forward and planted a kiss upon Cali's dark lips. Even with a mouth choked full of blood, the kiss was sweet, like monsoon rain after the arid heat of summer's wrath.

Then he twisted his blade and pulled it from her, bringing guts with it. Cali staggered back, collapsing against a pillar. Slowly, she began to slide down it, her legs no longer able to support her weight. She seemed terribly vulnerable: no longer the black goddess, merely a creature of flesh and blood, a wounded animal. She looked about her, blinking rapidly, and a strange expression of recognition stole over her face.

"Eric..." she murmured, blood spilling from her lips. Then she looked at LeBarron—or rather through him to the spirit that lay beneath: "A song . . . " she croaked. "About Eric . . . I promised him . . . "

Alan—or was it LeBarron—frowned, trying to understand her meaning.

"I deserve no song . . . " She wept tears so sparklingly real it was shocking. "But he . . . deserves a song."

"I will honour him," LeBarron said, at last grasping her meaning.

"Thank you," Cali whispered. Her eyes were star-bright.

Then she collapsed forward, dead.

An age later, the man who wore LeBarron's mask took two steps, turning to face the crowd that still waited—stunned beyond words or even comprehension—at the foot of the palace steppe.

"A song shall be composed in honour of Eric the courtier, and the other fallen dead," he declared. "The Claw of Craving shall be cast into the Fires of Manifestation and unmade . . . " He took a shuddering breath. "The two nations of the Eternal Enclave and Carcosa shall become one, ruled by our new Empress Cassilda—*Everlasting Her Name.*"

Then he fell down, as though he had been struck by God's own hand.

At last, the spell of paralysis was lifted. Cassilda and Petruccio stood, rushing up the steps towards the fallen warrior.

Cassilda knelt by his side. Petruccio stood behind her, his face a shadow of grief.

"LeBarron, what you just did . . . " Cassilda said. "It is beyond words, beyond gratitude. You have saved Carcosa."

"I tell you truly," he replied. "I am not LeBarron. I am Him."

Cassilda would not permit herself to weep.

"No." She shook her head. "It cannot be." She saw the grisly claw-mark in his stomach. "Let me tend your wounds, LeBarron." She reached out a hand, but he caught it, returning it gently to her side.

"My wounds are fatal, Cassilda. I tell you again: I am Him."

Cassilda would not weep.

"A thousand plays shall be written about you, LeBarron," Petruccio said. "You shall become the most famous man in all the black planet!"

"I tell both of you, I am not LeBarron." He reached up and touched Cassilda's face with his left palm. *"I am Him."*

Cassilda broke and wept, at last allowing herself to believe what she had secretly always known to be true. Like Penelope welcoming home the long-wandering Odysseus, she threw herself about his neck, sobbing uncontrollably into his chest.

"He's there, isn't he?" Cassilda said, tears streaming down her face. "There behind your eyes. Let me see him. Take off the mask."

He smiled, one final time.

"I wear no mask."

Cassilda blinked away her tears, unsure what he meant.

LeBarron's eyes were closing, fluttering, like butterflies unsure of their flowery perch.

"No," she whispered. "If you die, Carcosa dies, remember?" She was hysterical, her voice broken. "You are the dreaming. You're all that sustains it!"

With the feeble movement of his hand he pointed at his wound, from which blood copiously flowed, watering the palace steps like the altar of a sacrificial temple, running down into the city, a river of brilliant crimson, the beating lifeblood of a new artery.

"It was always meant to be this way," he whispered. "The way of sacrifice makes man whole. But one last task . . . " LeBarron pushed his fingers into the gory wound, and withdrew them bloodied. "Petruccio. Come forward."

The dwarf leaned in close, trembling.

"Here is thy sacrament, thy reward, deserved more than any soul in Carcosa."

"What do you mean?" Petruccio was breathless.

"The smallest piece of the dreaming will be yours forever."

The artist's eyes widened. A momentary doubt seemed to take hold, then Petruccio opened his mouth, and LeBarron lowered his fingers to the dwarf's tongue. A flash and crackle, like an electrical discharge. Petruccio recoiled, his head lolling back. He gazed heavenward, panting stertorously, eyes glowing. Then at last he lowered his gaze back to LeBarron, a serenity making his face seem like that of another man, of an inner god.

"Thank you, Alan..." he whispered. The serenity departed, like a banished demon, and tears streamed down Petruccio's face. The stone visage was at last utterly cracked and broken.

Alan smiled using LeBarron's mouth. He peered down again at his wound, at the blood washing the steps of the palace.

"Don't go . . . " Cassilda said, trembling.

He touched her cheek once more, a caress of shocking tenderness.

"We will see each other again, in your father's garden . . . "

Her eyes widened.

"We'll be together?"

"Together," he said, and the sureness in his voice shook her to her bones. He swallowed down blood, and turned his eyes away from her, as though it would be too difficult for him to leave the world if he were to continue staring at her face. "With this, the city shall live eternally—for dream and dreamer are finally One."

Before she could say any more, a look of pure bliss twisted LeBarron's face—or perhaps it was not a face but a mask. His body shuddered as though in rapture; the spirit passed from him, and he was no more.

EPILOGUE
TEN YEARS LATER

A THENA MATHERS HAD followed all the signs to the secret lodge. She knew it was the right place because there was a car parked outside the alleyway that looked like it had stood there for a decade or more. Its metal was rusted, the windshield blackened with grime, shoots of weeds growing up through the tyres. Why the council had not had it removed was anyone's guess. She supposed it was legally parked, too old to steal, and no one had come to collect it. So there it'd stood, rusting and succumbing to the advances of the natural world, like a gravestone built of machinery. To her, it was not a gravestone, but rather the marker on a perilous mountain that indicated *someone* like her had been there before.

The alleyway might have been foreboding at night. The edifices of the surrounding flats were like many-eyed sentinels guarding some underworld realm; the dumpsters proved citadels for the teeming rat populations; and the eerie play of neon over the rain-slick brickwork invoked the image of acid trips and mushroom quests, two things Athena had experienced aplenty in her search for answers.

The alleyway curved teasingly away from sight. She drew her leather jacket more tightly about her as she followed its path. She thought she had dressed in enough layers for the Spring morning, but somehow the cold felt more biting here, as though winds were blowing in from another universe. Or so she hoped. There was nowhere left for her to go in this world. Everything had gone wrong.

At the end of the alleyway stood *The Black Star*. She'd heard it was once a brothel, where one was initiated into the occult via the means of sexual rites. That was from an online source who claimed to have been turned away after failing some kind of trial of initiation. He seemed to genuinely want the best for Athena, asking only that she give him a full account of what transpired if she passed the trial in return for his information. She had a journal in her inner pocket for that very purpose, though whether her "trip" would merely be another psychedelic affair, or something more profound, she did not at this stage know.

A shutter occluded the doorway to the establishment. Her heart thumped in her chest with the madness of Jack Torrence's axe, battering down the door to kill wife and child. She'd loved horror movies her whole life, right up until the moment she found herself *in* one. *The demon*—she shuddered, pushing the memory down the way a dying man held in their intestines when the stomach had been slit open. *Why were insides so eager to be outside?* That was the kind of horrifying thought her brain would turn over and over as a child, occasionally uttering out loud, and often getting a rebuke from her mother as a result.

Mother was six feet deep now and could not help her. Father was another story, one she was not ready to deal with.

Try as she might, she could not hold the memories in. She recalled the demon's whispers, his tongue, the way he made her do things to other people, and the word he said, over and over again, a pearl covered in excrement, a delicacy sprouting in the filth of his mind, a mind she'd been forced to share . . .

Carcosa, Carcosa, Carcosa . . .

She had to know what it meant.

She approached the shutter and rapped on the harsh metal. She heard movement behind, a small, dark figure scurrying about.

"Why do you come?"

Athena hesitated, but only for a moment.

"I need to know—to understand—are there such things as demons? And . . . and what is Carcosa?"

A second of silence, and then the shutter rose with an infernal screech, revealing to Athena's surprise a dwarf. His face looked like it had been hacked roughly from stone. His body was strong, though not in the way of a body-builder with bulging muscles. It seemed rather that his ligaments and bones had ossified to the point he had become a living mountain. He smiled at her with surprising tenderness.

"Welcome. My name is Petruccio."

"Athena," she said.

That seemed to amuse him.

"A goddess of wisdom?" He eyed her up and down, though she sensed not with lascivious intent, but rather the appraisal a military captain might give a new recruit. "In black boots, black jeans, and a black leather jacket, no less."

Athena smiled back.

"Even Athena must have had a goth phase."

He laughed, a sound that, like a dog's bark, was strangely warm to the ear despite its harshness.

He led her down a long series of steps and into a sumptuously furnished corridor. The walls were white and black marble, and instantly made her think of the High Priestess Tarot card, with the two pillars either side, one representing mercy and the other severity. She knew about Tarot cards from watching *Jojo's Bizarre Adventure*. Not the most orthodox way to study them, but she'd found the anime's explorations of the symbolic meanings surprisingly deep. *I have come to the right place,* she thought.

"The lady likes white and black," Petruccio said, noticing the direction of her gaze. "Black for mourning, for my lady still feels the pang of her love's loss." The way he said it made it seem the loss was also his. "And white, for the purity of new beginnings."

Athena nodded.

Petruccio led her down a series of corridors, and despite the beauty of the décor she could not help but think of passages in a labyrinth, the runnels of a rat's warren. They passed one particular piece of decoration that brought her up short, almost physically arresting her steps.

It was a painting, resembling Da Vinci's *Last Supper,* only this could only have been a last supper taking place in hell. The work was exquisite, showing a host of demons with elongated skulls all sat at a feast, along with several other strange figures. At the head of the table sat a demon with a crown. Despite how terrifying the demon's aspect was, the artist had rendered his face with a nobility that was breathtaking. By his left side sat a man whose face seemed a shimmer of a thousand other faces. On his right was a beautiful princess with golden hair, and flesh so pale she seemed translucent. There was a coal-black warrior who carried a shining banner. Then there was a dwarf, who resembled Petruccio—no, it had to *be* Petruccio, for the artist had perfectly captured his granitic, scarred visage. And lastly there was a figure strangest perhaps for how ordinary he seemed, a middle-aged man with dark hair and eyes sat at a table with these fantastical entities, like the only living soul at a feast for the dead. Yet, even he bore one strangeness, a curious talisman, glittering and gold, cruel and wondrous, a magical hand.

She had no idea how long she stared at the piece.

"I call it 'Necrodeipnon'," Petruccio said. "I think it is my greatest work."

Athena flinched. She had been so absorbed she forgot his presence.

"This is you then? And you painted it?"

"Yes."

"It's . . . stunning. Mesmeric."

"Thank you."

"Who is the man with the golden hand?"

Petruccio's face shadowed for a moment. He stood there a long time, staring at the painting, lost in the kingdom of the past.

"A great magician," he said at last. "Perhaps even the greatest. And a good friend." His voice was thick with emotion. "Come, my mistress awaits."

Athena nodded, though she was loathe to tear her eyes away.

She followed Petruccio down a further series of corridors, until they came to a sturdy looking door. The dwarf opened it.

"Wait here, a moment."

He slipped through the door, though did not shut it entirely behind him, allowing a blade of shadow—and voices—to leak through. Athena could not resist. She approached silently and listened.

"You're sure about this?" she heard the dwarf say.

"Yes," a female voice replied. "It's what Alan would have wanted: as many people as possible to know the beauty and horror of . . . But hush, I think she is listening."

Athena felt her body go cold. How did the woman in the chamber know? Was this truly magic?

"I shall fetch her."

The dwarf stepped out and smiled at Athena.

"You are awaited by my lady."

Athena nodded, trembling.

THE KING OF CARCOSA

The dwarf beckoned her over, swinging wide the door. Athena stepped within. And then she beheld the ruler of Lost Carcosa, the Queen in Black, the Lady of Sorrow, and the Empress of the Black Planet. In her right hand, the goddess held a sword of white fire, and in her left she held a golden wand. On her brow was a crown of yellow gemstones that blazed like festering stars. Her face was white as snow, terrible as thunder, and beautiful as the first ray of sun breaking the long darkness of night.

Cassilda smiled.

Athena knew she'd found what she was looking for.

"I am afraid," LeBarron said, as the world melted away. "Where shall my spirit go?"

"I tell you truly," Alan replied. "You shall be with me in paradise tonight."

In the garden, their flowers bloom—even now—upon the eternal Tree of Life.

Join Blood Bound Books
Newsletter for updates and
receive 20% off your next order at
www.BloodBoundBooks.com

ACKNOWLEDGEMENTS

There are too many people to thank for the existence of this series. Firstly, I must profusely thank S. C. Mendes and Joe Spagnola of Blood Bound Books for being brave enough to take on my madness and see it through to the end. Throughout this process, they have been supportive, dedicated, given insightful feedback, and provided me with amazing, life-changing opportunities—including a trip to America I shall never forget.

Secondly, I must thank Christa Wojciechowski—an incredible friend, writer, mentor, and soul. Without her encouragement, my courage would have failed to pursue the erotic current that drives this series to its spiritual conclusion.

There are now too many amazing reviewers and readers to thank by name. Just know that I love you all, count each one of you as a blessing from God, and am forever in your debt.

Lastly, I would once again like to thank Edward Kennard for furnishing me with so many ideas for the prehistoric inhabitants of Yhtill.

Of course, it was the marshes of Yhtill to which Mercurio, the disciple of Pc'kar, fled in the aftermath of the battle of the trueborn, bearing with him the secrets of flesh-craft thought lost with the death of the Demon King. It was there, in the depths of the baleful marshes, that he would establish his new laboratory of dark materials, hidden in the ruined labyrinth of Namtar's Temple. For long years, he would nurse his hatred and channel it into the pursuit of absolute mastery over life and death, over flesh and void, until such time as his rage could no longer be satisfied by the pursuit of knowledge, and instead must be satisfied by the pursuit of something far darker . . .

ABOUT THE AUTHOR

Joseph Sale is the critically acclaimed Amazon best-selling author of more than 30 books, including *The Book of Thrice Dead, Virtue's End, Dark Hilarity*, and *The Claw of Craving*.

Despite growing up in the Lovecraftian seaside town of Bournemouth, he now lives in Winchester (in the UK) with his wonderful family, where he obsesses over table-top RPGs, trading card games, book bindery, esoteric Christianity, and anime.

You can get a free book from him, as well as being kept up to date on all his mysterious doings, by signing up to his mailing list at: themindflayer.com

www.ingramcontent.com/pod-product-compliance
Lightning Source LLC
Chambersburg PA
CBHW051946170626
46808CB00007B/2501